Sir Percy Fitzpatrick

The Outspan

Tales of South Africa

Sir Percy Fitzpatrick

The Outspan
Tales of South Africa

ISBN/EAN: 9783744752589

Printed in Europe, USA, Canada, Australia, Japan

Cover: Foto ©Andreas Hilbeck / pixelio.de

More available books at **www.hansebooks.com**

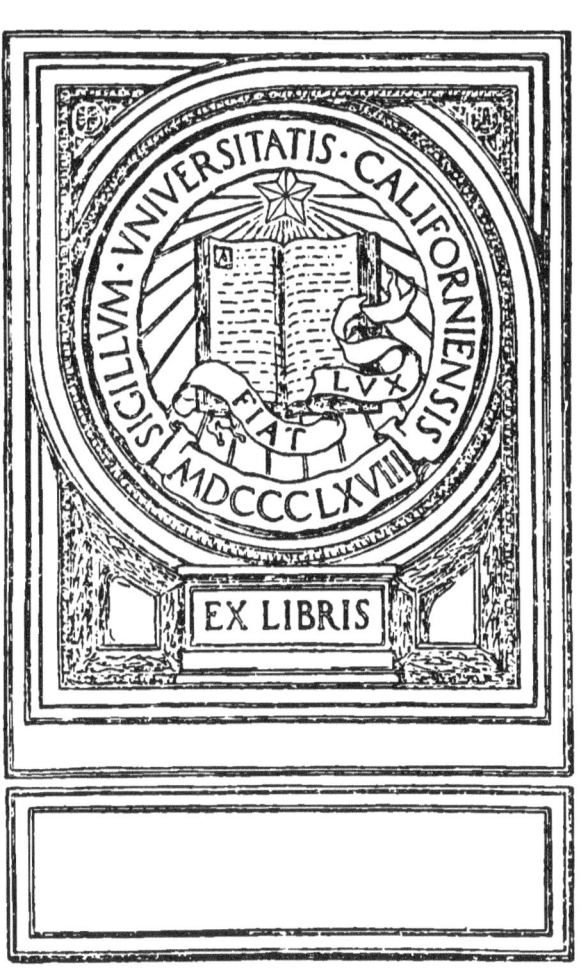

EX LIBRIS

THE OUTSPAN

Popular 3s. 6d. Novels.

A Pinchbeck Goddess. By ALICE M. KIPLING.
The Reds of the Midi. By FÉLIX GRAS.
Stories for Ninon. By EMILE ZOLA.
The Tower of Taddeo. By OUIDA.
The O'Connors of Ballinahinch. By Mrs. HUNGERFORD.
The Justification of Andrew Lebrun. By FRANK
    BARRETT.
A Comedy of Masks. By E. DOWSON and A. MOORE.
Appassionata. By ELSA D'ESTERRE-KEELING.
Eli's Daughter. By J. H. PEARCE.
Inconsequent Lives. By J. H. PEARCE.
Her Own Folk. By HECTOR MALOT.
Capt'n Davy's Honeymoon. By HALL CAINE.
A Marked Man. By ADA CAMBRIDGE.
The Three Miss Kings. By ADA CAMBRIDGE.
A Little Minx. By ADA CAMBRIDGE.
Not All in Vain. By ADA CAMBRIDGE.
A Knight of the White Feather. By TASMA.
Uncle Piper of Piper's Hill. By TASMA.
The Penance of Portia James. By TASMA.
The Copperhead. By HAROLD FREDERIC.
The Return of the O'Mahony. By HAROLD FREDERIC.
In the Valley. By HAROLD FREDERIC.
The Surrender of Margaret Bellarmine. By ADELINE
    SERGEANT.
The Story of a Penitent Soul. By ADELINE SERGEANT.
Nor Wife, nor Maid. By Mrs. HUNGERFORD.
The Hoyden. By Mrs. HUNGERFORD.
Mammon. By Mrs. ALEXANDER.
Daughters of Men. By HANNAH LYNCH.
A Romance of the Cape Frontier. By BERTRAM MITFORD.
'Tween Snow and Fire. By BERTRAM MITFORD.
Oriole's Daughter. By JESSIE FOTHERGILL.
The Master of the Magicians. By ELIZABETH STUART
    PHELPS and HERBERT D. WARD.
The Head of the Firm. By Mrs. RIDDELL.
A Conspiracy of Silence. By G. COLMORE.
A Daughter of Music. By G. COLMORE.
According to St. John. By AMÉLIE RIVES.
Kitty's Father. By FRANK BARRETT.
A Question of Taste. By MAARTEN MAARTENS.
Come Live with Me and Be my Love. By ROBERT
    BUCHANAN.

LONDON : WM. HEINEMANN, 21, BEDFORD ST., W.C.

TALES OF SOUTH AFRICA

BY

J. PERCY FITZPATRICK

LONDON
WILLIAM HEINEMANN
1897

CONTENTS

NOTE.—FOR THE ORIGINALS OF
CERTAIN CHARACTERS.

A person of my acquaintance was once
referred to in an up-country newspaper as
'Mr. Chimmage.' He wrote to the editor,
explaining that his name was not 'Chimmage,' but 'Schimmelovitch'; and the editor
in making the correction added, 'He has
only himself to blame for the fact being
known.'

J. P. F.

THE OUTSPAN.

'*THERE is no art in the Telling that can equal the consummate art of the Happening!*'

It was a remark dropped by a forgotten someone in a prospector's hut one night, years and years ago, when we had exhausted snakes and hunting, lucky strikes and escapes, and had got away into coincidences. One of the party had been telling us an experience of his. He was introduced on the day he arrived to a man well known on the fields. It seemed quite impossible that they could have met before, for they compared dates and places for ten years back, and yet both were puzzled by the hazy suggestion of having seen the other before, and, in our friend's case, of something more definite. His remark to the other was :

'I can't help feeling that I saw you once in a devil of a fright somewhere—or dreamt it, I suppose !'

But this first feeling faded quickly away, and

1

was utterly forgotten by both. Later on they shared a hut near Rimer's Creek, and afterwards, when houses came into vogue, they lived for several years together, while the first impression was lying buried, but not dead.

One day, in the process of swapping yarns, the other man was telling of the 'narrowest escape he ever had'—and all due to such a simple little mistake. A ticket-collector took the tickets at the wrong end of a footbridge. Instead of collecting them as the passengers from the train *went on to* the bridge, he took them as they were *going off*. The result was that the crowd of excursionists was too great for the little bridge, and it slipped between the abutments, carrying some two hundred people into the river below, the narrator being one of them. It was then that the dormant idea stirred and awoke—jumped into life—and our friend put up his hands as he had done fifteen years before, when the little bridge in Bath dropped, and gasped out:

' My God ! you were the other chap that hung on to the broken rail ! *That's* where we met !'

That was what prompted the forgotten one to say after we had lapsed into silence :

' There's no art in the Telling that can equal the consummate art of the Happening !'

And I only recall the remark because it must be

my apology for telling plain truth just as it happened.

* * * * *

When a man has spent some years of his life—the years of young manhood they generally are—in the veld, in the waggon, or tent, or Bush, it is an almost invariable rule that something which you can't define germinates in him and never entirely dies until he does. When this thing—this instinct, feeling, craving, call it what you will—awakens, as it periodically does, it becomes a madness, and they call it trek-fever, and then, as an old friend used to say, 'You must trek or burst!' There are many stories based on trek-fever, but this is not one of them; and if you were to ask those who know them, or, better still, get hold of any of the old hands, hard-headed, commonplace, unromantic specimens though they might be, who have lived in the veld—if you gave them time to let it slip out unawares—you would find that every man jack of them would have something to say about the camp-fire. I do believe that the fascination within the fascination is the camp-fire in veld life, with its pleasant yarn-swapping, and its long, pregnant, thoughtful silences, no less enjoyable. The least loquacious individual in the world will be tempted to unfold a tale within the circle of a camp-fire's light.

Everything is so quietly, unobtrusively sociable, and subjects are not too numerous in the veld, so that when a man has something *apropos* or interesting to tell, he commands an appreciative audience. Nobody bores, and nobody interrupts. Perhaps it is the half-lazy preference for playing the listener which everyone feels that is the best security against bores and interruptions.

The charm of the life is indescribable, and none who have tasted it ever weary of it, ever forget it, or cease to feel the longing to return when once they have quitted it.

It was in '91, the year after the pioneers cut their way through the Bush, with Selous to guide them, and occupied Mashonaland. We followed their trail and lived again their anxious nights and days, when they, a small handful in a dense Bush, at the mercy of the Matabele thousands, did not know at what hour they would be pounced on and massacred.

We crossed the Lundi, and somewhere beyond where one of their worst nights was passed we outspanned in peace and security, and gossiped over the ruins of ancient temples and the graves of modern pioneers. There were half a dozen of us, and we lay round the fire in lazy silence, too content to speak, simply *living* and drinking in the indescribable glories of an ideal African night.

It was someone knocking his pipe out and asking for the tobacco that broke the long silence, and the old Barbertonian, who had had to move to release the tobacco, looked round with the air of wanting someone to talk to. As no one gave any sign, he asked presently :

'Are you chaps asleep ?'

'No !' came in clear, wakeful voices, with various degrees of promptness.

'I was just thinking,' he said, refilling his pipe slowly, 'that this sort of thing—a night like this, you know, and all that—although it seems perfection to us, isn't really so perfect after all. It all depends on the point of view, you know. A night like this must be a perfect curse to a lion or a tiger, you know.'

'Your sympathies are too wide, old man,' said the surveyor. 'Chuck me a light, and console yourself that your predatory friends do well enough when others are miserable. Take a more human view.'

'If you want an outlet for your native sympathy, you might heave me out a cushion,' suggested another. 'I've made a pillow of a bucket, and got a dent in my head. The thick cushion, old boy, and I'm with you so far as to say that the lions have a jolly hard time of it with so much fine weather.'

The Barbertonian lighted up his pipe and threw the cushion at the last speaker.

' H'm !' he grunted between puffs. ' I was really thinking of it from quite a human standpoint—the view of that poor devil who got lost here two months ago. Now, *he* couldn't have thought much of nights like these. Do you think he mused on their beauty?'

' Oh, I heard something of him,' said one. ' Lost for forty days in the wilderness, wasn't he ? I remember. The coincidence struck me as peculiar.'

' Yes, it was odd in a way. He was just "forty days and forty nights." He went out with a rifle and five cartridges to kick up a duiker along the river bank here, and somehow or other got astray towards sundown, and lost his head completely. Five cartridges, seven matches, no grub, no coat, no compass, and no savvey ! That's a fair start for a forty days' picnic, isn't it ?' he resumed. ' Well, he fired off all his cartridges by dark, trying to signal to his camp, and then threw away his rifle. Fact ! He broke the heads off two matches—he was shaking so from fright—before he realized that there were only seven altogether. But as he had nothing to cook, it didn't really make much difference whether he had matches or not.'

' What, in winter time, and with lions about ?'

'*Yah!* Well, you get used to that. It was a bit frosty, and sometimes wet, and at first the lions worried him a lot and treed him several nights; but he says that that was nothing, while the sense of being lost—dead, yet alive—remained. What's that? Live? Oh, he doesn't know himself how he lived, but we could pretty well tell by his condition when we found him. We were out shooting about five miles down-stream, and on one of the sandy spits of the river we saw fresh footprints. Nigger, we thought, as it was barefoot. We wondered, because there were no kraals near here, and we had seen no cattle spoor or footpaths. I was on top of the bank every minute expecting a duiker or Bush buck to make a break out, and—I tell you—I don't know when I got such a start—such a *turn*, I should say—as when I caught sight of a white face looking at me out of an ant-bear hole. Great Cæsar! there was something so infernally uncanny, wild, and hunted in the look that I instinctively got the gun round to cover him if he came at me. When the others came up, he crawled out, stark naked, sunburnt, scratched, shock-headed — still staring with that strange hunted look—came up to us and—laughed! We led him back to our camp. He could tell nothing, could hardly understand any of our questions. He was quite dazed. His hands were cut and disfigured, the nails were worn off with burrowing for roots. We went to his den. It was a big ant-bear hole under an old tree and among rocks—a well-chosen spot. He had burrowed it out a bit, I think, and in a sort of pigeon-hole or socket in the side of it there were a few nuts, and round about there were the remains of nuts and chewed roots, stones of fruit, and such things. I never could understand how it was that, being mad as he certainly was then, he had still the sense—well, really it was an instinct more than any knowledge —to get roots and wild-fruits to keep body and soul together !'

' A suggestive subject, truly,' said a man who had more millions to his credit than you would expect of a traveller in Mashonaland. ' A man starving within rifle-shot of his friends and supplies. Helpless in spite of the resources that civilization gives him, and saved from absolute death by a blessed instinct that we didn't know was ours since the days of the anthropomorphic ape ! H'm ! You're right, Barberton ! He couldn't have thought much of the beauties of the night, and, if he thought at all, he must have placed a grim and literal interpretation on the *Descent* of Man when he was grubbing for roots with bleeding, nail-stripped fingers or climbing for nuts without a tail to steady him !'

Among us there was a retired naval man, a clean-featured, bronzed, shrewd-looking fellow, who was a determined listener during these camp-fire chats ; in fact, he seldom made a remark at all. He sat cross-legged, with one eye closed—a telescope habit, I suppose—watching Barberton for quite a spell, and at last said, very slowly, and seemingly speaking under compulsion :

'Well, you never know how they take these shocks. We picked a man up once whose two companions had lain dead beside him for days and days. Before he became delirious, the last thing he remembers was getting some carbolic acid from a small medicine-chest. His mates had been dead two days then, and he had not the strength to heave them overboard. I believe he wanted to drink the carbolic. Any way, he spilt it, and went off his head with the smell of carbolic around him. He recovered while with us—we were on a weary deep-sea-sounding cruise—but twice during the voyage he had short but violent returns of the delirium and the other conditions that he was suffering under when we found him. By the merest accident our doctor discovered that it was the smell of carbolic that sent him off. Once— years after this—he nearly died of it. He had had fever, and they kept disinfecting his room ; but, luckily for him, he became dangerous and violent, and they had to remove him to another place. He was all right in a few days.'

'Do you believe that a man could live out a reasonably long lifetime in the way that "forty days" chap lived ? I suppose he *could*, eh ? Shoo ! Fancy forgetting the civilized uses of tongue and limbs and brain ! It seems awful, doesn't it ? and yet men have been known to deliberately choose a life of savagery and barbarism—men whose lines had been cast in easy places, too !'

'That's all very well,' said Barberton. 'Now you are speaking of fellows settling down among savages and in the wilds voluntarily, and with certain provisions made for emergencies, etc., not of men *lost.*'

'Even so, a man must deteriorate most horribly under such circumstances.'

'Well,' said Barberton contemplatively, 'I don't know so much about that. It all depends upon the man. Mind you, I do think that the end is always fiasco—tragedy, trouble, ruin, call it what you like. We can't throw back to barbarism at will. For good or ill we have taken civilization, and the man who quits it pays heavy toll on the road he travels, and, likely enough, fetches up where he never expected to.'

The man who wrote for the papers smiled.

'I know,' he said with kindling eye—'I know.

It was just such a case you told us of at Churchill's Camp the other night. A man of the best calibre and training goes wild and marries two—mark you, *two!*—Kaffir women, and becomes a Swazie chief, and then the drama of the——'

'Drama be damned!' growled Barberton. 'It was one case out of twenty of the same sort.'

Barberton was nervously apprehensive of ridicule, and hated to be traded and walked out for effects.

'I was up on the Transvaal-Swazie border in '86,' said the millionaire. 'I remember you told me something of them then. It was a warm corner, Swazieland, then—about the warmest in South Africa, I should think. Eh?'

'You're right. It was. But,' said Barberton, turning to the correspondent, 'you were talking of men going *amok* through playing white nigger. Well, I can tell you this, that two of my best friends have done that same trick, and I'd stake my head that better men or more thorough gentlemen never trod in shoe-leather, for all their Kaffir ways.'

'Do you mean to say,' asked the millionaire, 'that you have known men settle down among natives, living among them as one of themselves, and still retain the manners, customs, instincts, habits of mind and body, even to the ambitions, of a white man?'

'No—well, I can't quite say that. Their ambitions, as far as you could gauge them, were a Kaffir's; that is, they aspired to own cattle, and to hunt successfully, but—— And yet I don't know that it is right to say *that* even, because in almost every case these men get the "hanker" for white life again sooner or later. The Kaffir ambition may be a temporary one, or it may be that the return to white ways is the passing mania. Who knows, any way? From my own experience of them, I can say that the return to their own colour almost invariably means their doom and ruin. I don't know why, but I've noticed it, and it seems like—like a sort of judgment, if you believe in those things.'

'And you know,' he said, after taking a few pulls at the pipe again, 'there's a sense of justice in that, too. Civilization, scorned and flouted, being the instrument of its own revenge! If one could vest the abstract with personal feelings, what an ample revenge would be hers at the sight of the renegade —sick-hearted, weary, and shamefaced—coming back to the ways of his youth and race, and succumbing to some one part of that which he had despised and rejected *in toto!*'

Barberton generally became philosophic and reminiscent on these fine nights. Someone would make a remark of pretty general application, and

he would sit up and wag his old head a few times
in silence ; then, from force of habit, examine his
pipe and knock it out on the heel of his boot, and
then out would lounge some reminiscence in illustration of his philosophy.

It was generally introduced by a long-drawn,
thoughtful, ' We-ll, you know, I've always thought
there was something curious about these things.'
He would have another squint down the empty
bowl of the pipe and ask for the tobacco. There
would be a couple of grunts, and then, as he lighted
up, he would say, between puffs, ' I remember, in
'78, up at Pilgrim's,' or, ' There was a fellow up
Barberton way in '86.'

This night he sat in tailor fashion, with an elbow
socketed in each knee-bend, and his hands clasped
over the bowl of his pipe.

' One of the rummiest meetings I ever had,' said
he, smiling thoughtfully at the recollection, ' was
in the Swazie country in '85. Did I ever tell you
about Mahaash and the Silver Spur ?'

He gave a gurgling sort of chuckle, and puffed
contentedly at the big-bowled briar.

' There were two of us riding through the Swazie
country, and making for the landing-place on the
Maputa side. We had had a row with the Portuguese about some cattle that the niggers stole from
us. A couple of the niggers got shot, of course,

during the discussion, and we had to quit for a
while and take a rest on the Lebombo. But that's
nix ! When we got to the Komati, we were told
that there was a white man on the Lebombo whose
Kaffir name was Sebougwaan. That's the name
the niggers give to a man who wears an eyeglass
or spectacles. We were jogging along doing our
thirty miles a day, living on old mealies roasted on
a bit of tin, and an occasional fowl—Swazie fowl,
two to the meal—helped down by bowls of amazi
—thick milk, you know. We used to sleep out in
the Bush every night, with a blanket apiece and
saddles for pillows, and the horses picketed at our
heads. Man, it was grand on nights like this ! We
were always tired and often hungry ; but to lie there
in the peace and stillness of the Bush, to look up
at the stars like diamond dust against the sky, and
not care a damn for anything in God's world, why
—why—I call that living ! All those months we
had no knowledge of the outer world. As far as
we were concerned, there might as well have been
none. We had one book, "The Ingoldsby Legends."
If anyone could have seen me reading Ingoldsby
by the light of the fire, and have heard every now
and then the bursts of laughter over " The Jackdaw
of Rheims " or " The Witches' Frolic," and others,
his face would have been a study, I expect.

  ' However, I was telling you about Mahaash.

Mahaash was a big induna, and had about five to seven thousand fighting men. He used to konza to Umbandine, but paid merely nominal tribute, and was jolly independent. He was the cleverest-looking nigger I have ever seen. Small, thin, and ascetic-looking, with wonderfully delicate hands, clear features, and lustrous black eyes. Really, he gave one the idea that he saw through everything, or next to it, and though he said very little, he looked one of the very determined quiet ones. We had to pass his place to get to Sebougwaan's, and, of course, had to stay the day and pay our respects. His kraal was on top of the highest plateau, near the Mananga Bluff. It lay on the edge of a forest, and the road—an aggregation of cattle-tracks—was very steep and very stony. You can imagine we were not overflush just then, and what puzzled us was what to give the chief as a present when he would accord us an interview. Rifles and ammunition we daren't part with, and we were mortally afraid they were just the things he would want to annex. Finally, it occurred to us to present him with one of my chum's silver spurs. Heron didn't favour this much. He said it would likely cause trouble ; but I put that down to his disinclination to spoil his pair of swagger spurs. Only the day before our arrival the chief had purchased a horse ; he had sent to Lydenburg for it, and it was the first they had ever seen in that part of the country—which seems odd when you think that the chief's own name, Mahaash, means "the Horse." However, to proceed. We got word next day that the chief would see us, and after the usual hour's wait we had our indaba, and presented the silver spur. I must say he viewed it very suspiciously—very!—and when we showed him how to put it on, he gave a slow, cynical smile, and made some remark in an undertone to one of his councillors. I began to agree with Heron about the unwisdom of giving a present so little understood, and would gladly have changed it, but that Mahaash—who was of a practical turn of mind—sent a man for our horses, and bade us ride with the "biting iron" on. We gave an exhibition of its uses which pleased him, and we, too, felt quite satisfied—for a moment! But things didn't look quite so well when he announced that he was going to ride his horse, and he desired Heron to strap the spur on to his bare foot. It was no use hesitating —we had to trust to luck and the chances that a skinny moke such as his was would take no notice of a spur ; besides which Heron, with good presence of mind, jammed the rowels on a stone and turned most of the points. It was no good, however. The chief had never been astride a horse before; he was hoisted up by a couple of stalwart warriors. Once on, he laid hold of the mane with both hands, and gripped his heels firmly under the horse's belly. I saw the brute's ears go flat on his neck. The two supporters stepped back. Mahaash swayed to one side, and, I suppose, gave a convulsive grip with the armoured heel. There was a squeal and scuffle, and a black streak shooting through the air with a red blanket floating behind it. The chief bounced once on the stony incline, shot on for another ten feet, and fetched up with his head against a rock. I can tell you that for two minutes it was just hell let loose. We dropped our rifles—we always carried them—and ran to the chief. I believe if we had kept them they'd have stuck us, for there were scores of black devils round each of us, flashing assegais in our faces, and yelling: "Bolalile Inkos! Umtagati! umtagati!"—"They have killed the chief! Witchcraft! witchcraft!" But in another minute we saw Mahaash standing propped up by several kehles, and holding one hand to his head. He steadied himself for a moment, gave us one steady, inscrutable look, and walked into his private enclosure.

'For four days we remained there—prisoners in fact, though not in name. Nothing was said about leaving, but our guns and horses were gone, and we were given a hut to ourselves in the centre of the kraal. We didn't know whether Mahaash was

2

dead, dying, or quite unhurt. We didn't know whether we were to be despatched or set free, or to be kept for ever. On the morning of the fifth day we found our horses tied to the cattle kraal in front of our hut, and a gray-headed induna brought word to us that Sebougwaan, for whom we were looking, lived not far from there along the plateau. We took the hint, and saddled up. As we were starting an *umfaan* brought a kid, killed and cleaned, and handed it to me—a gift from the chief; and the old induna stepped up to Heron with a queer look in his wrinkled, cunning old phiz, and said :

'"The chief says, 'Hamba gahlé' ('Pleasant journey'), "and sends *you* this."

'It was the silver spur.'

Barberton had another squint at his pipe, and chuckled at the recollection of the old nigger's grim pleasantry.

'But I was telling you about that white man on the Bomba,' he resumed. 'Well, we weren't long in making tracks out of Mahaash's kraal, and as we dodged along through the forest, following a footpath which just permitted a man on foot to pass, we realized how poor a chance we'd have had had we tried to escape. Every hundred yards or so we had to dismount to get under overhanging boughs or trunks of fallen trees or networks of monkey-ropes. The horses had got so used to roughing it that they went like cats, and in several places they had to duck under the heavy timber that hung, portcullis fashion, across the dark little pathway. This was the only way out at the back of Mahaash's. In front of him, of course, were the precipitous sides of the Lebombo Range.

' We went on for hours through this sort of thing, hardly seeing sunlight through the dense foliage ; and when we got out at last into a green grassy flat, the bright light and open country fairly dazzled us. Here we met a few women and boys, who, in reply to our stock question, gave the same old reply that we had heard for days : " Sebougwaan ? Oh, further on ahead !"

' We just swore together and like one man, for we really had reckoned to get to this flying Dutchman this time without further disappointments. We looked around for a place to off-saddle, and made for a koppie surrounded by trees.

' Heron was ahead. As we reached the trees, he pulled up, and with a growing grin called to me, " I say, just look here ! Here's a rum start !"

' It was clearly our friend Sebougwaan. He was standing with arms akimbo, and feet well set apart, surveying critically the framework of a house he was putting up.

' He had a towel round his loins, and an eyeglass screwed tightly into the near eye. Nothing else.

'We viewed him *en profile* for quite awhile, until he turned sharply our way and saw us. It was one of the pleasantest faces in the world that smiled on us then. Sebougwaan walked briskly towards us, saying :

' " Welcome, gentlemen, welcome. It's not often I see a white face here. And, by-the-by, you'll excuse my attire, won't you ? The custom of the country, you know, and 'In Rome——' Well, well. You'll off-saddle, of course, and have a snack. Here, Komola ! Bovaan ! Hi, you boys ! Where the devil are they ? Here, take these horses and feed them. And now just 'walk into my parlour.' Nothing ominous in the quotation, I assure you."

' He bustled us around in the jolliest manner possible, and kept up a running fire of questions, answers, comments, and explanations, while he busied himself with our comfort.

' It was a round wattle-and-daub hut that he showed us into, but not the ordinary sort. This one was as bright and clean as a new pin. Bits of calico and muslin and gay-coloured kapelaan made curtains, blinds, and table-covers. The tables were of the gin-case pattern, legs planted in the ground ; the chairs ordinary Bush stools ; but what struck me as so extraordinary was the sight of all the English periodicals and illustrated papers laid out in perfect order and neatness on the table, as one sees them arranged in a reading-room before the first frequenters have disturbed them. There was also a little hanging shelf on which were five books. I couldn't help smiling at them—the Bible, a Shakespeare, the Navy List, a dictionary, and Ruff's Guide.

'They say that you may tell a man by his friends, and most of all by his books; but I couldn't make much out of this lot, with one exception. I looked at the chap's easy bearing, the pleasant, hearty manner and torpedo beard, and concluded that the Navy List, at any rate, was a bit of evidence. However, he kept things going so pleasantly and gaily that one had no time in which to observe much.

'Lots of little things occurred which were striking and amusing in a way, because of the peculiar surroundings and conditions of the man's life rather than because of the incidents themselves. For instance, when we owned up that we had had no breakfast, we found ourselves within a few minutes enjoying poached eggs on toast, and I felt myself grinning all over when the Swazie boy waited in passable style with a napkin thrown carelessly over one shoulder. Surely a man must be a bit eccentric to live such a life as this in such a place and alone, and yet take the trouble to school a nigger to wait on him in conventional style.

'I thought of the peculiar littleness of teaching a nigger boy that waiter's trick, and concluded that our friend, whatever his occupation might be, was not a trader from necessity. After breakfast he produced some excellent cigarettes—another fact in the nature of a paradox.

'We were making for the landing-place on the Tembe River, and had intended moving along again that day; but our host was pressing, and we by no means anxious to turn our backs on so pleasant a camp, so we stayed overnight, and became good friends right away.

'I was quite right. He had been in the navy many years, and had given it up to play at exploring. He said he had settled down here because there was absolute peace and a blissful immunity from the ordinary worldly worries. Once a week a native runner brought him his mail letters and papers, and, in fact, as he said, he was as near to the world as he chose to be, or as far from it.

'He had a curious gold charm attached to a watch-chain, which I saw dangling from a projecting wattle-end in the dining-hut. I was looking at this, and puzzled over it; it seemed so unlike anything I had ever seen. He saw me, and, after

putting us to many a futile guess, told us laughingly that he had found it in one of the villages
they had sacked on the West Coast. I don't know
what sort of part he took in these nasty little wars,
but I'll bet it was no mean one. We listened that
night for hours to his easy, bright, entertaining
chat, and although he hardly ever mentioned himself or his own doings, one couldn't but see that he
had been well in the thick of things, and dearly
loved to be where danger was. Now and then
he let slip a reference to hardships, escapes, and
dangers, but only when such reference was
necessary to explain something he was telling us
of. What interested us most was his description
of General Gordon—"Chinese Gordon"—with whom
he appeared to have been in close contact for a
good while. The little details he gave us made up
an extraordinarily vivid picture of the soldier-saint,
the man who could lead a storming-party, a forlorn
hope, with a Bible in one hand and a cane in the
other ; the man who, in the infiniteness of his love
and tenderness, and in the awful immutability of
his decision and justice, realized qualities in a
degree which we only associate with the Deity. I
felt I could see this man helping, feeding with his own
short rations, nursing, and praying with, the lowliest
of his men, the incarnation of mercy. But I also
saw him facing the semi-mutinous regiment of

barbarians, and, with the awful passionless decision
of fate itself, singling out the leaders here and there
—in all a dozen men—whom he shot dead before
their comrades, and turning again as calm and unmoved as ever to repeat his order, which this time
was obeyed ! I pictured this man, with the splendid
practical genius to reconquer and reorganize China,
treasuring a cutting which he had taken from what
he verily believed to be the identical living tree
from which Eve had plucked the forbidden fruit.
Surely, one of the enigmas of history !'

'Do you mean to say that's a fact ?' asked the
millionaire, as old Barberton paused.

' As far as I know, it certainly is. Our friend
told it as a fact, and not in ridicule, either, for he
had the deepest reverence and regard for Gordon.
He assured us, moreover, that Gordon was once
most deeply mortified and offended by a colleague
of his treating the matter as a joke and laughing
at it. Gordon never forgot that laugh, and was
always constrained and reserved in the man's presence afterwards.

' I wish I could remember a hundredth part of our
host's anecdotes of well-known people, descriptions
of places and of peoples, accounts of travels and
adventures. He seemed to know everyone and all
places. It was three in the morning before we
thought of turning in. After breakfast we saddled

up and bade adieu, but our friend walked along part of the way with us to put us on the right path. He was carrying a bunch of white Bush flowers—a curious fancy, I thought, for a man clothed in a towel and an eyeglass. I remarked on the beauty of the mountain flowers, and he held up the bunch.

' " Yes," ' he said, " they are lovely, aren't they ? Poor old Tarry ! He was my man—the only other white man that ever lived here. He was with me for many years, and died here two summers back —fever contracted on the Tembe. Poor old fellow ! I fixed him up on the bluff yonder. He used to gather these flowers and sit there every day of his life looking out towards Delagoa, wondering if we would ever quit this place and get a sight of old Ireland again. I take him a bunch once in a while. Come up and see where a good friend lies."

' We left the horses and climbed up the rough path, and looked at the unpretentious stone enclosure and the soft slate slab with a rough-cut inscription :

> "PADDY TARRY'S REST !
> *Are ye ready ?*
> *Aye, aye, sir !*"

' Our friend leaned over the low stone wall and replaced the faded wreath by the fresh one.

' We left him standing there on the ridge, clear-

cut above the outline of the mountain, and took
our way down the rough cattle-path that wound
down to the still rougher, wilder kloof through
which our route lay. I remember so well the way
he was standing, one foot on a projecting rock,
arms folded, until we were rounding the turn that
took us out of sight. Then he waved adieu.

*   *   *   *   *

' We had unpleasant times on that trip to the
Tembe. We met all the murderous ruffians in
that Alsatia, and they were all at loggerheads,
thieving and shooting with both hands. However,
we got out all right after months and months of
roaming about, owing to the trouble about those
Kaffirs, and I think we had both forgotten all
about Sebougwaan by the time we fetched up in
Lydenburg again. There was always something
happening in that infernal outlaw corner of Swazieland to keep the time from dragging !

' My chum went off to his farm ; but I had no
home, and took the road again with waggons, and
loaded for Barberton at slashing fine rates. I got
there just as the Sheba boom was well on. Companies were being floated daily, shares were booming, money flowing freely. All were merry in the
sunshine of to-day. No one took heed of to-morrow.
Speculators were making money in heaps ; brokers
raking in thousands.

'You know how it is in a place like that. After you have been there for a few hours, or a day or two, you begin to notice that one name is always cropping up oftener than any other; one man seems the most popular, important, and indispensable. Well, it was the same here. There was always this one name in everything—market, mines, sport, entertainment—any blessed department. You can just imagine—at least, you can't imagine—my surprise when I found that my naked white Kaffir sailor-friend, Sebougwaan, was the man of the hour. I couldn't believe it at first, and then a while later it seemed to be the most natural thing in the world; for, if I ever met a man who looked the living embodiment of mental, moral, and physical strength, of good humour, grace, and frankness—a born king among men—it was this chap.

'I met him next day, and he seemed more full of life and personal magnetism than ever. After that I didn't see him for three or four days; you know how time spins away in a wild booming market. Then somebody said he was ill—down with dysentery and fever at the Phœnix. I went off at once to see him. I couldn't believe my eyes. He was emaciated, haggard, with black-ringed eyes sunk into his head, and so weak that he couldn't raise his arm when it slipped from the bed. He spoke to me in whispers and gasps, only a word or two,

and then lay back on the pillows with a terrible
look of suffering in his eyes, or occasionally dropping the lids with peculiar suddenness ; and when
he did this the room seemed empty from loss of this
horrible expression of pain.

' I stood at the foot of his bed, and didn't know
what to do or say, and didn't know how to get out
of a room where I was so useless. This sort of
thing may only have lasted a few minutes, or
perhaps half an hour—I don't know ; but after
one long spell he opened his eyes suddenly and
looked long and steadily into mine, sat bolt upright,
apparently without effort, lifted his glance till I felt
he was looking over my head at something on the
wall behind me, and then raised both arms, outstretched as though to receive something, and,
groaning out, "Oh, my God! my poor wife!"
dropped back dead.'

      *   *   *   *   *

There were five intent faces upturned at Barberton as he stopped. The rosy glow of the fire
lighted them up, and the man nearest me—the
millionaire—whispered to himself, ' Good God !
how awful !'

' Well, who was he ? Did you——' began the
man who wrote for the papers.

Barberton looked steadily at him, and with
measured deliberation said :

'We never knew another word about him. From that day to this nothing has ever been heard to throw the least light on him or what he said.'

Far away in the stillness of the African night we heard the impatient half - grunt, half - groan of the lion. Near by there was a cricket chirping; and presently a couple of the logs settled down with a small crunch, and a fresh tongue of flame leaped up. Barberton pumped a straw up and down the stem of the faithful briar, and remarked sententiously :

'Yah, it's a rum old world, this of ours! I've seen civilization take its revenge that way quite a lot of times—just like a woman!'

No one else said a word. Now and then a snore came from under the waggon where the drivers were sleeping.

The dog beside me gave some abortive whimpers, and his feet twitched convulsively—no doubt he was hunting in dreamland. I felt depressed by Barberton's yarn.

     *   *   *   *   *

But round the camp-fire long silences do not generally follow a yarn, however often they precede one. One reminiscence suggests another, and it takes very, very little to tempt another man to recall something which 'that just reminds him of.'

It was the surveyor who rose to it this time ; I

could see the spirit move him. He sat up, stroked
his clean-shaven face, closed the telescope eye, and
looked at Barberton.

'Do you know,' he began thoughtfully, 'you
talk of chaps going away because of something
happening—some quarrel or mistake or offence or
something. That is all a sort of clap-trap romance,
I know—the mystery trick, and so forth; but I
confess it always interests me, although I know it's
all rot, because of a thing which happened within
my own knowledge—an affair of a shipmate of
mine, one of the best fellows that ever stepped
the earth, in spite of the fact that he was a regular
Admirable Crichton.

' He was an ideal sort of chap, until you got to
know him really well, and found out that he was
cursed with one perfectly miserable trait. He
never — absolutely *never* — forgave an injury,
affront, or cause of quarrel. He was not huffy
or bad-tempered — a sunnier nature never was
created ; a more patient, even-tempered chap never
lived—but it was really appalling with what im-
mutable obstinacy he refused to forgive. In the
instances that came under my own notice, where
he had quarrelled with former friends—not through
his own fault, I must say—nothing in this world,
or any other, for that matter, could influence him
to shake hands or renew acquaintance. His gener-

osity and unselfishness were literally boundless, his courage and fidelity superb ; but anyone who had seen evidence of his fault must have felt sorrow and regret for the blemished nature, and must have been awestruck and frightened by his relentlessness. Death all round him, the sight of it in friends, the prospect of it for himself, never shook his cursed obstinacy ; as we knew, after one piece of business. He got the V.C. for a remarkable—in fact, mad—act of courage in rescuing a brother officer. The man he carried out, fought for, fought over, and nearly died for, was a man to whom he had not spoken for some years. God knows what the difference was about. This was their first meeting since quitting the same ship, and when he carried his former friend out and laid him safely in the surgeon's corner of the square, the half-dead man caught his sleeve, and called out, "God bless you, old boy !" All *he* did was to loosen the other's grip gently, and, without a word or look at him, walk back into the fight. It seems incredible—it did to us ; but he wouldn't know him again. He had literally wiped him out of his life !

'This trait was his curse. He was well off and well connected, and he married one of the most charming women I have ever met. For years none of us knew he was married. His wife was, I am convinced, as good as gold ; but she was young,

attractive, accomplished, and, in fact, a born con-
queror. Perhaps she was foolish to show all the
happiness she felt in being liked and admired.
You know the long absences of a sailor. Well,
perhaps she would have been wiser had she cut
society altogether; but she was a true, good
woman, for all that, and she worshipped him like a
god! None of us ever knew what happened; but
he left wife and child, settled on them all he had
in the world, handed over his estates and almost
all his income, and his right to legacies to come,
went out into the world, and simply erased them
from his mind and life.

'That was a good many years ago—ten, I should
think; and—I hate to think it—but I wish I was
as sure of to-morrow as I am sure that he never
recognised their existence again.'

The surveyor shuddered at the thought.

'He was a man who could do anything that
other men could do. He was best at everything.
He was loved by his mates, worshipped by his
men, and liked and admired by everyone who met
him—until this trait was revealed. Others must
have felt as I did. When I discovered *that* in
him, I don't know whether I was more frightened
or grieved. I don't know that I didn't stick 'to
him more than ever—perhaps from pity, and the
sense that he was his own enemy and needed help.

I have never heard of or from him since he left the service, and yet I believe I was his most intimate friend. Oliver Raymond Rivers was his name. Musical name, isn't it ?'

Barberton dropped his pipe.

' Good God ! Sebougwaan !'

SOLTKÉ.

AN INCIDENT OF THE DELAGOA ROAD.

WE were transport-riders trekking with loads from Delagoa Bay to Lydenburg, trekking slowly through the hot, bushy, low veld, doing our fifteen to twenty miles a day. The roads were good and the rates were high, and we were happy.

Towards sundown two of us strolled on ahead, taking the guns in hopes of picking up a guinea-fowl, or a stembuck, or some other small game, leaving the waggons to follow as soon as the cattle were inspanned. We shot nothing; in fact, we saw nothing to shoot. It was swelteringly hot, as it always is there until the red sun goes down and all things get a chance to cool. It was also very dusty—two or three inches of powdery dust under our feet, which whipped up in little swirls at the least breath of air. I was keeping an eye on the scrub on my side for the chance of a bush pheasant, and not taking much notice of the road, when my

companion pulled up with a half-suppressed exclamation, and stood staring hard at something on
ahead.

'Dern my skin !' said he slowly and softly, as I
came up to him. He was a slow-spoken Yankee.
' Say, look there ! Don't it beat h—ll ?'

In the direction indicated, partly hidden by the
scant foliage of a thorn-tree, a man was sitting
on a yellow portmanteau reading a book. The
sight was unusual, and it brought the unemotional
Yankee to a standstill and set us both smiling.
The man was dressed in a sort of clerk's everyday
get-up, even to the bowler hat, and as he sat there he
held overhead an old black silk umbrella to protect
him from such of the sun's rays as penetrated the
thorn-bush. He must have become conscious of
the presence of life by the subtle instinct which we
all know and can't explain, for almost immediately
he raised his glance and looked us straight in the
eyes. He rose and came towards us, laying aside
the umbrella, but keeping his place in the book.

The scene was too ludicrous not to provoke a
smile, and the young fellow—he could not have been
above twenty-three—mistaking its import, raised
his hat politely and wished us ' good-afternoon.'

He spoke English, but with a strong German
accent, and his dress, his open manner, his ready
smiles, and, above all, his politeness, proclaimed

him very much a stranger to those parts. Key murmured a line from a compatriot : ' Green peas has come to market, and vegetables is riz.'

' You have come mit der waggons ? You make der transport ? Not ?' he asked us, following up the usual formula.

We told him it was so, and that we were for the fields, and reckoned to reach Matalha by sun-up. He too, he said, was going to the gold-fields, and would be a prospector ; he was just waiting for his ' boy,' who had gone back for something he had forgotten at the last place. He was going to walk to Moodie's, he said. He ' *did* make mit one transporter a contract to come by waggons ; but it was a woman mit two childs what was leave behind, and dere was no more waggons, so he will walk. It was good to walk to make him strong for de prospect. Oh yes !'

We were used to meeting all sorts on the road, and they were pretty well all inclined to talk ; but this one was so full it just bubbled out of him, and in his broken English he got off question on ques-tion, between times imparting scraps of information about himself and his hopes. He was clearly in earnest about his future, and he was so utterly unpractical, so hopelessly astray in his view of everything, that one could not but feel kindly towards him. We chatted with him until our

waggons came up, when he again politely raised
his hat as he said good-bye to us, and offered many
thanks for the information about the road. As we
moved on with the waggons, he turned to look
down the road by which we had come, and said,
apparently as an afterthought :

'You haf seen my " boy " perhaps ? Not ? No !
Soh ! Good-bye—yes, good-bye !'

It does not take long for daylight to glide
through dusk into darkness in the bush veld in
South Africa, and even these few minutes spent in
conversation had seen the light begin to fade from
the sky as the sun disappeared. The road was
good and clear of rocks and stumps, so we hopped
onto the most comfortable waggon, and talked
while the oxen plodded slowly along.

We had quite a large party that trip, for, besides
Gowan and myself, who owned the waggons, we
had three traders from Swazie country—old friends
of ours who had come down to Delagoa to buy
goods. We had all arranged to stand in together
in a big venture of running loads through Swazieland to the gold-fields later on in the season ; in
fact, the trip we were then making was more or
less a trial one to see how the land lay, and how
much we could venture in the big coup.

Gowan, the other transport-rider, and I always
travelled together. We were not partners exactly,

but in a country like that it was good to have
a friend, and we understood each other. There
were no two ways about him ; he was a white
man through and through. The two Mackays
were brothers ; they had left Scotland some
years before to join a farming scheme 'suitable for gentlemen's sons with a little capital,' as
the circular and advertisements said. They had
given it best, however, and gone trading long
before I met them. The other member of our
party was the one with whom I had been walking.
He was an American, and had been everything and
everywhere, most lately a trader in Swazie country.
We generally called him the Judge.

As the waggons rumbled along Key was giving
a more or less accurate account of our conversation
with the stranger.

It was very amusing, even more amusing than
the original, for I am bound to say that with him a
story did not suffer in the telling. It was only
Gowan who didn't seem to see anything to laugh
at in the affair. He sat there dangling his legs
over the buck-rails, chewing a long grass stalk,
and humming all out of tune. He had a habit of
doing that, growling with it. Presently, as conversation flagged, the tune got worse and his growling
took the shape of a reference to 'giving a poor
devil a lift.'

I frankly confessed that I simply had not thought of it, and that was all. As, however, Gowan continued growling about 'beastly shame' and 'poor devil of a greenhorn,' etc., Key answered dryly.

'Waal, I *did* think of it; but, first place, they ain't my waggons——'

Gowan grunted out, 'Dam rot!'

'And second place,' continued Key placidly, 'considerin' the kind o' cargo you've got aboard, and where it's going to, I didn't reckon you *wanted* any passengers!'

'I don't want passengers,' said Gowan gloomily; 'but any d——d fool knows that that fellow 'll never see food or blankets or " boy " again on the face of God's earth. Kaffir carriers don't forget things at outspans. No, not any that I've seen, and I've seen a good few.'

Old Gowan took up the grass stem again, and chewed and tugged at it, and made occasional kicks at passing bushes, by way of showing a general and emphatic disapproval. No one said anything; it was Gowan's way to growl at everything, and nobody ever took much notice. He was the most good-natured, kindly old growler that ever lived. He growled as some sturdy old dogs do when you pat them—they like it.

In this particular case, of course, he had reason

It is not that we were inhospitable or unfeeling, but years of roughing it had, I suppose, dulled our impressions of the first night alone in the veld, and we had not seen it as Gowan did. Life of the sort we led, no doubt, develops the sterling good qualities of one's nature, but quick sympathy and its kindred delicate traits are rather growths of refinement and quiet, and it betrayed no real want of feeling that we had not taken Gowan's view.

There could be no doubt, of course, that the Kaffir boy had bolted with the blankets and food, for we had noticed that the young German had nothing left when we saw him but that yellow portmanteau, and our knowledge of the Delagoa Bay 'boy' forbade acceptance of the theory that he had gone empty-handed.

We rumbled heavily along for a bit, and after a while Gowan resumed, in a tone of deeper grumbling and more surly dissatisfaction than before :

'Like as not the silly young fool'll lose himself looking for water, and die in the Bush, like that one Joe Roberts brought up last season. Why, I remember when——'

'Grave o' the Prophet !' exclaimed Robbie, starting up in mock alarm ; 'he's going to tell us that dismal yarn about the parson chap who hunted beetles, and was found after a week's search with two of his most valuable specimens feeding on his

eyes. Skip, sonnie, skip ! and fetch up your German
friend 'fore the old man gets under way.'

Key dropped off the buck-rails, as the drivers
shouted their 'Aanhouws' to the cattle to give
them a breather, kicked his legs loose a bit, dusted
down his trousers quietly, and, smiling good-
humouredly at Gowan, 'guessed it was better
business to hump that gripsack a mile or two than
listen to old Yokeskey's prayers.' That was his ir-
reverent way of alluding to Gowan's calling of transport-rider—a yokeskey being part of the trek gear.
Key and I set out together at a brisk pace, well
knowing how poor was our chance of catching up
to the waggons again before the midnight outspan.

Key, who was always tickled by Gowan's
growling tones, remarked after we had walked for
some minutes :

'Sling hell like a nigger parson, you know, can
the old 'un, but soft and harmless as a woman.'

After half an hour's brisk walking, we caught
the unsteady flicker of a fire through the straggling
thorns, and we found our friend sitting tailorwise
before it, making vigorous but futile attempts to
wisp aside the smoke that would go his way. His
look of mild curiosity at the sound of our voices
wakened up into welcome when he recognised us,
and he at once became interested in the reason of
our return.

'You haf lose something—not? I, too, will
look for you,' he said, jumping up eagerly; but we
reassured him on that point, and inquired in turn
whether his 'boy' had returned, and cross-ques-
tioned him as to the when and wherefore of his
leaving.

The Kaffir-bearer, he said, had left him that
morning during the after-breakfast trek.

'Ten hours gone, by Jimmie!' muttered the
Judge.

'And you have waited here since then?' I asked.

'Oh yes, yes! I read to learn de English. It
is——'

'Had any scoff?'

'Please?'

'Had any grub—anything to eat or drink?'
explained Key, illustrating his meaning by graphic
touches on mouth and belt.

'No, no; I am not hunger. Also it is good
that I eat not. It make me use for the prospect.'

Key smiled gently, and said, with a quaint
judicial air :

'Waal, I don't know as that's quite necessary;
but ef you kin stick it out till that nigger o' yours
comes back, I guess you'll do for most any camp
you'll strike in this country. Say! Has he got
the blankets? Yes! And the grub? So! An'
—er—mebbe you didn't give him money as well?'

'I haf give him one pound to pay the passport, which he forgot. He say policeman will take him if he shows not the ticket. But he will come bring to me the change. He is ein goot boy, and he speaken English feul goot; but perhaps something can happen, and that policeman haf take him, I think.'

Even in a new-comer such credulity was a revelation. I could not help smiling, but the Judge's clear-cut, impassive features never changed; only, at the mention of the 'boy's' lingual accomplishments, he winked solemnly at me.

The Judge brought matters to a practical issue by telling our friend that he 'had much better wait at our waggons for the good boy that speaks English so well.'

'It ain't,' said Key, 'es if he couldn't find you. A Kaffir kin find you most anywhere if he wants to—'specially them English-speakin' ones,' he added, with a twinkle in his eyes.

Key did not wait for any reply, but turned the 'yaller gripsack' over and looked at the name, 'Adolf Soltké,' painted in big white letters.

'Your name?' he asked in chaff, rather than that he doubted it.

'My name, yes. Soltké—Adolf Soltké—coom from Germany, but in der colonie I was leetle times.'

'Took you for Amurrikan,' said the Judge, without a vestige of a smile.

I looked hastily at Soltké, feeling that his broken, halting English should have protected him from such outrageous fooling, but my solicitude was misplaced. Soltké calmly, but firmly, disclaimed all knowledge of America, and repeated that he was a German.

Key shouldered the portmanteau with the curt suggestion, ' Waal, let's git !' and as our friend— except by his protestations of gratitude and wild endeavours to carry the whole of the kit himself— offered no hindrance to the proposed scheme, we marched along briskly to overtake the waggons.

A bullock-waggon is a slow one to travel with, but a bad one to catch, as anyone knows who has tried it ; and it was close on midnight when, tired and dusty, we came suddenly on the waggons out-spanned in a small opening in the Bush.

The silence was absolutely ghostly, except when now and then a bullock would give a big long sigh, or a sappy stick in the fire would crack and hiss.

Gowan was sitting over the fire on a three-legged rough-wood stool, head in hands and elbows on knees, with the odd jets of flame lighting up his solemn old face and shaggy brown beard. The others had turned in. He stood up slowly as we

came up and extended a hand to Soltké, saying
baldly :

'How are ye ?'

Our friend took the inquiry in a literal sense,
and was engaged in answering it, when Gowan cut
in with a remark that it was 'time to be in bed,'
and, accepting his own hint, he hooked his finger
in the 'reimpje' of his camp-stool and strolled off
to where his blankets were already spread under
one of the waggons.

As he turned, he pointed with his foot to the fire,
growling out that there was a billy of tea and some
stew warmed up 'for him' (looking back at Soltké),
and adding, 'Bread's in the grub-box. 'Night !'
he turned in.

It was just like him to remember these things,
for in our routine there was as a rule no eating
during the night outspan.   It was breakfast after
the morning trek, and supper before the evening
one.   Gowan had also thrown out a couple of
blankets, and between us we made up pretty
well for the lost bedding ; so Soltké was installed
as one of the party.   It says something for him
that, in spite of our eight-mile walk and that
yellow portmanteau, the verdict under our waggons
that night was : 'Seems a decent sort, after all,
and it *would* ha' been a bit rough to leave him to
shift for himself.'

Soltké's stupendous greenness should have disarmed chaff; and, indeed, at first we all felt that fooling him was like misleading a child : there was no fun to be got out of it. He believed anything that was told him. He accepted literally those palpable exaggerations which are not expected or wanted to be believed. He took for gospel the account of the Munchausen of the Bush-veld who told how his team of donkeys had been disturbed by a lion during the early morning trek, and how, to his infinite surprise and alarm, he found that the savage brute had actually eaten his way into one donkey's place, and when day broke was found still pulling in the team, to the great dismay of the other members. He was anxious to make a personal experiment of the efficacy of dew taken off a bullock's horn, which we had recommended as an infallible snake charm. At considerable risk he had secured the dew, and the scene of Soltké's struggling with the bewildered bullock at early dawn one morning was one to be remembered. However, he pledged himself not to carry the experiment further without the assistance of one of us, and a day or two later we removed immediate risk by losing his phial of dew. I am convinced that he would have tried the experiment on any snake he might have met, and with absolute confidence as to the result.

His mind was such as one would expect in a
child who had known neither mental nor physical
fear. He seemed absolutely void, not only of
personal knowledge of evil, but even of that cogni-
zance of its existence which shows itself in a disposition to seek corroborative evidence, to consult
probabilities, and to inquire into motives. I am
convinced that Soltké never questioned a motive in
his life, nor ever hesitated to accept as a fact anything told in apparent seriousness. Irony and
sarcasm were to him as to a child or a savage. He
was intensely literal, single-minded and direct, and
perfectly fearless in thought, word or act. Such a
disposition in a child would have been charming.
In a well-set-up, active young man of three-and-
twenty or so it was embarrassing. Donald Mackay,
who was of a choleric disposition, complained a day
or two after Soltké joined us that ' he was blanked
if he could blank well stand it. Why, that morning, when he was about to gi'e one o' the boys a
lambastin', the kiddie turns white as a girl wi' the
first swear and a sight of the sjambok, an' Aa tell
ye, mon, Aa was nigh to bustin' wi' a' the drawing-
room blether Aa was gettin' off.' It was quite
true. Soltké was not shocked nor affecting to be
shocked at the vigorous language he heard; he
was simply unlearned in it, and shrank as a girl
might from the outburst of violence.

Gradually the feeling of strangeness wore off, and the restraint which the new presence had imposed was no longer felt except on odd occasions. On our side, we chaffed and shook him up, partly on the impulse of the time, and partly with good-natured intent to make him better fitted to take care of himself among the crowd with whom he would mix later on. On his side, he had never felt restraint, and of course rapidly became familiar with us and our ways, and seemed thoroughly to enjoy the chaff and his initiation into the system of good-humoured imposture. With all his green-ness, he was no fool; in fact, he was in odd, un-expected ways remarkably shrewd and quick, as he often showed in conversation. He was, moreover, a poor subject for practical jokes, and several of the stock kind recoiled on the perpetrators, because, as I have said, he did not know what fear was.

When a notorious practical joker named Evans, with whom we travelled in company for a couple of days, ' put up ' the lion scare on Soltké, it didn't come off. He asked our young friend to dine at his waggons on the other side of a dry donga, and, after telling the most thrilling lion yarns all the evening, left Soltké to walk back alone, while he slipped off to waylay him at the darkest and deepest part of the donga. There was the rustle of bushes and sudden roar which had so often played havoc before ; but Soltké only stepped back, and lugged out in unfamiliar fashion a long revolver which no one knew he carried. Ignoring the fact that a lion could have half eaten him in the time expended, Soltké calmly cocked the weapon, and, to the terror of his late host, poured all six barrels into the bush from which the noise had come. He then retreated quietly out of the donga to where we, hearing the shots and Evans's shouts of terror, had run down to see what was up. Soltké was excited, but quiet, and the noise of the reports had evidently prevented him from detecting the man's voice. He said :

'It was something what make "Har-r-r-!" by me, and I shoot ; but I haf no more cartridge.'

We did not see Evans again for some months. The story of Soltké's lion made the road too hot for him that winter.

When we told Soltké the real facts, his face was a study. For some days he was very quiet and thoughtful ; he was completely puzzled, and for the life of him could not imagine the motive that had actuated Evans ; nor could he, on the other hand, realize the possibility of anyone acting differently from the way in which he had done.

Before this there had been some horseplay when we were crossing the Komatie River. The stream was running strong, and was then from four to five

feet deep at the drift ; and, although it was known
to be full of crocodiles, there was little or no danger
at the regular crossing.   However, Key had primed
Soltké with some gorgeous stories of hairbreadth
escapes, intending to play a trick on him in the
river.

'It is quite a common thing for men to be carried
off here,' said the Judge ; 'but white men are very
seldom killed—not more than four or five a year—
because of the boots.'

'Boots !' exclaimed Soltké inquisitively.

'Yes,' said Key, in half-absent tones.   'Ef you
kick properly, no croc' can stand it.'

Soltké complained excitedly, and as though he
had suffered gross injustice, that no one had told
him this interesting phase of life on the road ; but
Key snubbed him, telling him that men didn't
speak much of such matters, as it gave the impression of bragging.

Soltké, who was above all things desirous of
conforming with the etiquette of the road, asked
no more questions ; but Key, later on in the
day, affecting to relent a little, got Soltké to sit
straddle-legs on the pole of one of the waggons,
and there, under his directions, practise kicking
crocodiles.

The crossing was too difficult for one span of
oxen, so we double-spanned, and put all hands on

with whips and sjamboks along the thirty oxen, to whack and shout until we got through.

Key placed himself behind Soltké and, just when the excitement was greatest, with his long whip-stick and lash he made a loop, in which he managed to enclose Soltké's legs. One jerk took him clean off his feet, and down-stream he went, floundering and kicking for dear life, for he believed a crocodile had him. His kicking when he was head downwards and his legs were free of the water was remarkable. There were roars of laughter from everyone, as Key had passed the word along; but presently there was a lull, and the niggers stopped laughing and felt the joke fall flat, when Soltké, utterly unconscious of the real cause of his upset, waded deliberately back as soon as he recovered his feet, and, pale but undaunted, took his place, sjambok in hand, the same as before.

Among transport-riders the condition of the Berg—as the spurs of the long Drakensberg range of mountains are called colloquially—is always a fruitful topic of conversation. The Berg at Spitz Kop is worse than at any other point, I believe, and Soltké exhibited a growing interest in this much-discussed feature of the road. His enthusiastic nature led him here into all sorts of speculations about it, which were highly amusing to us; and the Judge egged poor Soltké on and crammed

4—2

him so that he undertook in our interest to devise
some method for ascending this awful Berg
whereby the then terrible risks to life and property
would be minimized, if not entirely removed. The
position, as Key explained it, was this : There was
a long, steep hill to be surmounted, the grade of
which varied between 30° and vertical, but the
crowning difficulty lay in the 'shoot.' Here it
was an open question whether the hill did not
actually overhang ; so steep was it, in fact, that it
was not an uncommon occurrence for the front oxen
to slip as they gained the summit, and fall back
into the waggon, possibly killing both leader and
driver, and doing infinite damage to the loads.
Soltké faced this problem brimful of confidence in
the subject and himself. After hours of keen discussion and diligent experiments, Soltké produced
his plan. It was a system of endless rope on guides
and pulleys, so arranged that by a top anchorage
on the summit of this hill both oxen and driver
would be secure. Soltké was triumphant, but Key
extricated himself temporarily by pointing out that,
as we had not enough rope to try the scheme, we
would have to take the old roundabout road and
leave the 'shoot' for the next trip.

The joking with Soltké, as I have said, at times
degenerated into common horseplay, and this led
to the only unpleasantness we had. The younger

Mackay—Robbie—was a quiet, humorous, and most gentle-natured fellow, an immense favourite with everybody.

One night we were all standing round the fire, when something occurred which nobody ever seemed able to explain. Soltké had mislaid his pipe, and, thinking he had seen Robbie take it, asked him for it back. Robbie denied all knowledge, and Soltké, deeming it but another practical joke, said, 'I saw you taking it, you ——,' using a term which he, poor chap, had picked up without knowing the meaning, a term which among white men never passes unnoticed. Robbie's Scotch blood was aflame, and before one of us could stir, before he himself could think of the allowances to be made, before the word was well said, a heavy right-hander across the mouth dropped Soltké back against the waggon. Blank amazement and something like consternation marked every face, but none was so utterly taken aback as poor Soltké, who would have suffered anything rather than inflict pain upon a fellow-being. He only said, 'Robbie, what haf I say? I do not understand,' and, looking white and miserable, walked quietly off to his blankets and turned in. To us it was as though a girl, a child, had been struck, and no one felt this more than Robbie himself, as soon as he saw that the insult was not intentional. The look on Soltké's face was that of a stricken woman, a look of dull, unmerited pain. He was not cowed — just dazed and hurt, but inexpressibly hurt. You will see men blink and shuffle under that look in a woman's face. You will see a master quail before it in a servant. You will see White go down before it in Black ; for it is God's own weapon in the hands of helpless right. As long as I live I shall remember that look. I felt as though I had done it !

We trekked as usual next morning at about three o'clock, and it must have been some time in the dark hours of the early trek that Robbie spoke to Soltké. Whatever it was he said, it relieved the awkwardness, and restored Soltké to something of his old self ; but he was never quite the same again, and for some days we did not get over the look in his eyes and the feeling of guiltiness it left in us.

Robbie did not speak of that early morning scene, but later in the day remarked incontinently :

' By God ! he is white, is Soltké—white all through.'

Soltké kept a diary, and kept it with the most marvellous fidelity and unflagging industry, and he also learned to shoot, and shot cockyolly birds occasionally, and was pleased to know their sporting and scientific names. There is a sort of bastard cockatoo in those parts which is commonly known

as the ' Go way ' bird, on account of its cry, which
closely resembles these words, and of a habit it is
supposed to have of warning game of the approach of
man. In Soltké's diary there should be an elaborate
essay on the ancestry and personal habits of this bird,
and the wonderful traditions of its family. He
took these things down faithfully and laboriously
from the Judge's own lips. The Judge had a
copious mythology. Poor Soltké tried to stuff
some of his dicky-birds, labelling them with such
names as Key could always supply at a moment's
notice. The result was unpleasant, as Soltké took
to bestowing these ill-preserved relics in the side-
pockets of the tents, in the waggon-boxes, and in
a dozen other unlikely spots. It was only now and
then that we could actually find them ; but there
was a constant suggestion of their proximity, nevertheless.

We took to calling Soltké the Professor, as it
was a title which, we told him, seemed better to
suggest an all-round efficiency than any other we
could think of, and therefore suited him more than
such purely departmental distinctions as Leather-
stocking, the Engineer, or the Ornithologist.

I had forgotten to say that there was one thing
on which we did not chaff poor Soltké. He played
the zither. I do not know if he played it well or
not, for he was the only one whom I have heard

play that instrument. To us, lying round a bright thornwood fire, in which the big logs burnt into solid glowing coals—to us, who lay back smoking or gazing up into the infinite depths of silent, cloudless sky, watching millions and millions of stars twinkling busily and noiselessly down at us, the music was a kind of dream.

As Soltké sat in the glow of the fire, and the unsteady flicker of shooting and dying flames threw lights and shadows on his face, it sometimes looked as though he was not quite what we took him for. His was a bright, intelligent face, lit up by quick, eager blue eyes; in fact, though it was a thing that we took no stock in, Soltké was really a very good-looking boy, and one naturally thought of him as some 'mother's hope and pride'; and the look of worry and grief that I sometimes fancied I saw was put down to home-sickness brought out by music. However good or bad his music was, he seemed to feel it, and we—well, we never talked much after he began to play; and when he stopped, we generally knocked our pipes out with a sort of half-sigh, and turned in for the night. It used to make me think of home as I remembered it when I was still externally respectable—before I took to flannel shirts and moleskins, and ways that were not home ways; and I expect the others felt that too.

We had passed the Crocodile River and the belt
of 'Tsetse Fly' country. We had passed Josikulus,
where Hart was murdered by the niggers, and we
told Soltké the story of the dead man's sentry-go.
We passed Ship Mountain, and pointed out the
bush that hid the haunted cave, and told him the
weird tradition of the old witch-doctor imprisoned
by the rock slide, handling still as a skeleton the
implements of magic he used in life.

All these things were noted in Soltké's volumi-
nous diary ; and a curious medley it must have
contained, with the embroidered facings of Key
and the solid square facts of Gowan intermingled
with the author's own original remarks and reflec-
tions. Soltké, to do him justice, was clearly a
person of some purpose. He had placed before
himself an ideal, and he never lost sight of it. He
was eternally qualifying for that pursuit which he
called 'de prospect.' He would eat from choice the
charred and blackened crust of an overbaked loaf
or a steak that had slipped the gridiron and got
well sanded ; he also seemed to prefer the dregs
of the coffee billy, which he swallowed black and un-
sweetened; he scorned to use a fork; and he always
slept on the lumpiest ground ; and all this was to
fit him for the hardships and emergencies he
promised himself as a full-blown prospector. His
eagerness for knowledge of the flora and fauna was

equally remarkable : he had compiled a sort of
dictionary of plants and animals, describing their
virtues, medicinal or culinary, and I am sure that
towards the end of our trip Soltké would have set
out into the Bush with a light heart, armed only
with his book, and fortified by a confidence which
was absolutely phenomenal.

Looking back on it all, it seems a mean shame
ever to have played on his credulity ; and, indeed,
most of us were, even at this time, keenly alive
to this ; but there were times when his eager
questioning and intense earnestness about commonplace trifles made temptation irresistible, and
seemed even to inspire one with ridiculous notions
suited to Soltké's undiscriminating appetite.

It was on a Sunday morning that we came in
sight of Pretorius Kop—a solitary sugar-loaf hill
—and we lay by as usual during the hours of daylight. We knew it was Sunday, because Soltké
had said so, and because we saw him in the early
morning kneeling in the shadow of a big tree
a few yards from the waggons, Prayer-book in
hand, absorbedly following the prayers of the Mass.
He was a Roman Catholic, and was as uncom-
promisingly particular in observing the smallest
detail of his Church's ritual and teaching as he was
by nature tolerant of the shortcomings of others.
In the course of the morning's short excursion

Soltké had come across one of those crawling creatures known to children as 'thousand-legs,' the common, harmless millepede. It was the first he had ever seen, and words failed him in his quest for information. Key was the first he met on his return, and the Judge told him solemnly that the insect in question was 'that well-known and most ferocious of reptiles, the viper.' During breakfast Soltké absorbed whole volumes of information about this 'wiper'—its habits and uses, and as soon as the meal was over he betook himself to the side-pocket of the tent waggon, where the beloved diary was kept, and commenced to write up the new discovery. We were all spread about enjoying the morning smoke, or taking it easy in other ways. We had forgotten Soltké, but presently his face popped out, wearing a most worried, earnest, and intense expression.

'Joodge!' he called, 'Joodge, how vos dot wiper shpell?'

Key dictated calmly :

'W-h-y-p-e-r, whyper,' and Soltke with infinite pains put it down. But we heard him a moment later from his place in the tent of the waggon murmuring :

'Lieber Himmel ! dot vos un oogly name.'

He kept his diary in English, and many a perspiring hour did he spend in his struggles with our

language ; but he never quailed once, never even
slackened, for he said it was 'goot to make him
friends mit der English, and he can talk him when
he shall coom on der prospect.'

Soltké could hardly have taken down the name
of this new wonder, when the sight of a blue jay
flying past — one marvellous blaze of gorgeous
colour as its shiny feathers caught the sunlight—
sent him into a perfect paroxysm of excitement.
He had seen the honeysuckers, and knew them in
the diary as 'birds of Paradise'; he knew the
ordinary or cockyolly bird as the small 'pheasant
of Capricorn'; he had shot dicky-birds by the
dozen and stuffed them, and their noxious odours
seemed to add zest to his ornithological pursuits ;
but he had never seen, never dreamed of, anything
like this.   For one spellbound moment Soltké
watched the bird sail by, and then gasped out :

'Gott in Himmel! what woss dat ? Christnacht,
be shtill, und I shot him.'

Diary, pen, ink and blotter were thrust aside,
and Soltké scrambled for the gun.   We turned our
backs on him to watch the bird.   Soltké jumped
from the waggon.   The report of the two barrels
was so loud and close that it made us duck ; but
the blue jay sat unmoved.

There was a curious silence that made several of
us look round together.   The gun had fallen, and

Soltké was standing above it, rigid and ghastly white, with one hand gripping a burnt and blood-spattered tear in his right leg. As we sprang to him open-armed he seemed just to sway gently towards us with closed eyes and a soft murmur of words in his own tongue. It sounded like a prayer.

I think he fainted then; but we were never sure, as he was always so still with it all that one couldn't tell at times whether he was dead or alive. The medicines we had, and the remedies we knew, did not run to gunshot wounds and broken legs, but we made shift to fix him up somehow with a rough ligament.

It was here that Key came in. Quiet and self-possessed, firm and kind, he cut away the burnt, torn clothing. He washed out the ragged, black-ened wound; he tried the leg, and told us it was fractured—shattered—and would have to come off. And Soltké lay there, under the big tree, on a blanket spread on a heap of grass, as white as alabaster and as still, while we watched silently beside him, fanning him with small green boughs, and keeping off the flies.

Donald Mackay had started off at once for a doctor; but we knew that, with the best luck in finding him, and riding day and night, it must be over two days before we could get him down there.

Robbie went with his brother to the nearest
waggons a few miles on ahead, where Donald raised
a horse and went on alone on his long ride for help.
Robbie came back with a few things that we hoped
would help a little, and then we settled down to
watch in silence the awful race between ebbing
life and coming help.

Through the hot, long, quiet day we watched
and tended him, and so on into the cool of the
evening. We could do nothing, really; but it
seemed to please him and us to whisk away the
flies, and say a word of cheer to him, or now and
then to shift the cotton sheet that covered him.
When the stars came out, and the soft cool feel of
night grew up around, and the ruddy flicker of the
fire worked its magic on the encampment, changing
and beautifying everything with sudden lights and
weird shadows ; when the cattle were tied up to the
yokes, and one by one lay down to sleep with great
restful, deep-drawn sighs; when there were no
sounds but the steady chewing of the cud and the
occasional distant howl of a hyena or the sharp,
unreal laugh of the jackal—then did we really
seem to settle down to the business of waiting.

Now and then, perhaps three or four times in
the night, Soltké asked for water; once or twice
towards morning he sighed a suppressed tired sigh ;
but not a word of complaint, not a sign of im-

patience, not one evidence of the torture he was enduring, escaped him. When morning came, cool and fragrant, and the blue smoke of the camp-fire curled up straight and clean into the pure air, he was as quiet and uncomplaining still, though not for one second had his eyes closed nor the deadly numbing pain ceased its ache.

Soltké seemed to me to look younger than ever, though terribly white and fagged. His eyes looked blue and brave and trustful—childishly trustful—as ever, and he alone, of all the party, did not keep looking towards the west for the return of Donald Mackay and his charge.

All that day we watched and waited, and on through another slow and silent night; but we could see then that Soltké could not last out much longer without a doctor's help, and that his chance was becoming a poor one.

It must have been about three in the morning when, lying flat on my back, looking up into the wonderful maze of stars that spatters our southern sky, I heard or felt the tiniest tap, tap, tap under my head. I shot up with the cry of, 'There's Donald at last!'

We were all up and listening, but could hear nothing when standing, of course. However, there was no mistake, and after five minutes we could hear on the cool, clear, still air the footfall of a horse—*one* horse, as we all remarked with an awful heart-sinking.

Two of us—Key and I—went on to meet the horseman, and in a few minutes came upon Donald leading a horse, upon which, by the aid of a propping arm, was balanced a man whom we all knew —only too well.

In a breath Donald told us that he had sent on from the first camp for the district surgeon, but, chancing on Doc Monroe, had packed him on the horse and come back with him as a makeshift. Munroe was a quack chemist of morose and brutal character, and a drunkard with it. His moral status might be gauged by the fact that no patient among those who knew him personally or by repute ever approached him professionally except upon the contract system—so much the job, payment on delivery, cured. He had a certain repute for ability. God knows how it was earned, for he had killed more men than any other agency in the country; but I believe that his brutal and sardonic indifference to public opinion, his fiendish hints that there was no accident about the deaths of *his* patients, and that ' those who want Doc Munroe can pay for him, by G—d !' inspired a weird dread which, irrationally, perhaps, yet not unnaturally, begot a sort of blind awed belief in the man's ability.

Men hardly stricken have been known to sit on the bar-step and wait while Doc, having drunk himself drunk, would drink himself sober, and then, with implicit faith, swallow down mixtures to which the bloodshot eyes and the trembling hands of the Doc added the interest of a blind gamble.

By the uncertain light of the stars I had not recognised him, until Key, who was a few paces in front, said softly :

' It's Doc Munroe—dead drunk !'

Donald was utterly worn out, and wild with despair. Doc had been drunk when he found him, but (as Donald said) he was always that, and he had hoped that a forty-mile ride would sober him. However, it seems that twice on the road he had got liquor, and the second time, when Donald had caught him and taken it away, he had sat down by the roadside stolid and immovable until the liquor was returned to him.

There were reasons why we bottled up our rage and treated the Doc with a show of civility, and even conciliatory respect. We knew, firstly, that he had his instruments, and that only he could use them ; and, secondly, that, however drunk he might be, he never lost his senses until delirium set in ; and, moreover, that he was intensely suspicious of offence when in this state, and if once huffed, was indifferent to prayers and threats alike. The look on Gowan's face was positively murderous when he saw in what manner our waiting was rewarded. I am sure he would readily have killed Munroe at that moment.

Poor Soltké showed his first signs of anxiety then, and we had to make what excuses we could— the want of light, first of all, and then the long ride—to account for the doctor's not seeing him now that he had come. But the hours went by, the last chance was ebbing away, and we could do nothing—absolutely nothing—with the man.

We tried him with everything. We gave him black coffee—he wouldn't touch it; we tried soup —he kicked it over ; food, sleep, a bath—everything was rejected with a sullen and stolid shake of the head, and the one word ' W'isky.' That we would *not* give. For four mortal hours the man lay sullenly by the waggon on a pile of blankets, and only the one word passed his lips. We dared not give him more—it would have destroyed our only chance ; and without liquor he would not budge.

Day was well advanced when Munroe stood up quietly, and walked over to where Gowan stood beside his waggon. I suspected that the Doc had noticed Gowan's look when he came into camp with us, and now it was clear that he had.

' You think I'm drunk,' said Munroe, with a

malignant sneer. 'I saw you look at me when I got off that d——d horse! You think I'm drunk, do you?'

Gowan looked him steadily in the eyes, but made no answer, and Doc resumed :

'Are you going to give me that whisky?'

Again no answer ; but I walked nearer, as I could see Gowan's hands close and go back, and his chest came up with hard breathing.

'Are — you—going—to—give — me — that — whisky?' asked Munroe again, slowly and deliberately.

'No!' roared Gowan, with a tiger-like spring at the other man ; 'I'll see you in hell first!'

I caught Gowan's uplifted arm, but Munroe never flinched, and, pulling himself together with something of a shake, he said in a perfectly sober, even tone and with diabolical malevolence :

'Then I'll see your friend dead and rotten before I stir a hand to help him;' and with that he marched back to the blankets and lay down again.

An hour passed, and he never stirred a finger— never even blinked his staring eyes. Then the Mackays, Key, and I held a council, and decided to give him the liquor as a last—a truly forlorn— hope. It was left to me to see him, and I went over bottle and glass in hand.

He wouldn't touch it.

I argued, begged, and prayed ; but it had no effect whatever. He just lay there, resting on one arm, with the cruel, shallow glitter in his eyes that one sees in those of wild beasts. I returned to the others, and we had another talk, and then I offered him money—a price : all that we could give! That fetched him. He sat up, and looked at me for about a minute, and then said, shaking with hate :

'Your liquor I won't touch. Your money won't buy me. As soon as it's cool enough to move, I go back ; and if you've ever heard of Doc Munroe, you'll take that for a last answer.'

That was a facer, and when I went back and told the others, opinions were divided as to what to do. Gowan and Key were for the rifle cure. If he wouldn't operate, shoot him !

But we urged another—a last—delay, say till noon ; and they gave way, but warned us it would be useless.

The heat that day was awful. No breeze, no relief—only dead, oppressive heat, reflected to and fro the steel-blue sky and the hard-baked earth.

The fires were out—we had cooked nothing that day—and the camp looked dead and deserted. One or more of us would always be with Soltké ; the others would be lying in the shadow of a tree or under a waggon. We had some faint hope that the district surgeon would turn up, but not before the morrow, and, knowing Soltké's condition, that seemed useless, so that our only real chance was with Munroe.

As we lay there, dismally and hopelessly waiting, we were suddenly startled by a most peculiar and unnatural bark. The two dogs also jumped up and ran out on to the road. We could see nothing except that Munroe had gone. The noise was repeated, and the dogs growled, and every hair stood up on their backs.

'Great God! look there!' came from Donald.

Following his glance, we saw, low down amongst the thick buffalo grass, the wild, haggard face of Doc Munroe. His shock red hair half covered his eyes, which glittered and glared like a lioness's. As we stood he barked again, and made a jump out to the margin of the grass. He was mad—stark, staring mad—with delirium tremens! In one of his hands, half hidden by the grass, we could see a Bushman's friend, and the bright blade seemed to catch an ugly gleam from the man's eyes and reflect it malevolently back on us.

Munroe was a big man, and, although ruined in health by years of hard drinking, would have been a very ugly customer while the mad fit lasted; so we just stood our ground, ready to take him any

way he wanted to come. After a minute or two he
seemed to feel the effect of four pairs of eyes looking
steadily at him, and the wild beast died out, and
his body, which had been as rigid as a 'standing'
pointer's, became visibly limp and nerveless. He
got up heavily, with a silly, hysterical laugh, and
stood meekly before us, looking as foolish and
harmless as a human being might. He sidled over
towards Donald Mackay, keeping as far as possible
from Gowan, whom he clearly distrusted, and
looking furtively about, as though others besides
us might hear him, he said, with a sickly smile
and in a thin, uncertain voice :

'I was playin', Donald, old man, only playin'.
You know me—old Doc Munroe. *You* weren't
frightened, Donald, eh?   He! he!   I *like* to bark,
ye know.   I *like* it, and who'll stop me if I like it,
eh?   You could see I was playin', old partner.
You knew it, didn't you ?'

The man was wretchedly weak and shaky, and
as he continued to look about anxiously, he wiped
the heavy drops of cold perspiration off his colourless face with the dirty strip of kapalaan which
did service for a pocket-handkerchief. He sidled
up closer and closer to Donald, and watched with
growing intentness and terror the place from which
he had just emerged. Mackay quietly imprisoned
the knife-hand, but Munroe never noticed that,

and only clung closer to him, and began to mutter and cry out again, quivering with excitement and terror, which grew on him, until he shrieked to Donald to save him, and to ' knife him over there '—pointing to the tree beneath which he had hidden. Key took the proffered knife, and, walking quietly towards the tree, began to hack it in an unenthusiastic manner ; and the relief that this seemed to give Munroe would have been ludicrous but for the desperate hopelessness it brought for poor Soltké.

It was no longer possible to keep up our well-intended fiction about the doctor requiring rest, for Munroe's maniac laughter and shrieks of terror became so frequent and awful that they must have startled one half a mile away. He became so violent that we were obliged to take him down to the spruit, and to tie him down there in the shadow of a high bank, with one of the niggers to look after him, and an occasional visit from one of us to see if all was well.

Soltké bore the news as he had borne all that went before, with silent, martyr-like patience. He seemed to have guessed it : not a muscle moved, not a feature changed. He listened to it as calmly as he listened to our expressed hope that the district surgeon would turn up by sundown, and with as little personal concern.

Towards evening he spoke a good deal to us all, but in a way that made our hearts sink. He spoke of his home and his past life—for the first time—and of something that was troubling him greatly. He also admitted that his leg was feeling very hot, and that he felt twinges of pain shooting up into the groin and body.

At sundown he asked for his Prayer-Book, and later on, when we had left him alone for a while, and sat in silent, helpless despair by the neglected fire, he asked for Robbie. At last, at about ten o'clock that night, we heard the welcome sound of a horse's trotting, and to our unspeakable delight the cheery little doctor turned up. Poor old Soltké did brighten up then, and the smile which had never failed him throughout the days of suffering seemed to me more easy and hopeful. In less than an hour the shattered leg was off. In spite of the bad light and the rude appliances all went well, and with infinite relief we saw Soltké doze off under the merciful influence of the morphia which the doctor had brought. We felt that we had rounded the turn, and could afford to sleep easy. The little doctor, who had ridden seventy miles since sun-up, rolled into his blankets near where Soltké slept, and was in the land of dreams long before we, who were restless from very relief and joy, could settle down to close our eyes.

I seemed to have dozed for but a few minutes, when in my dreams, as it seemed to me, I heard in the faintest but clearest whisper the doctor saying : 'Mortification, you know! I couldn't see it by candle-light, or we might have spared him the operation.'

He was just dead. He sighed himself out, as the doctor said, like a tired child to sleep. We buried him close to the road under a big thorn-tree, which we stripped of its bark for a couple of feet to serve for a headstone for his grave. It was the tree where we had seen him on his knees at prayer. And as it neared sundown, we called for the oxen, and inspanned for the evening trek.

The doctor had gone. He had to get back those seventy miles to see another patient, whose life perhaps depended upon the grit of his gallant little horse.

During the night Munroe had managed to get loose, and with a madman's cunning had got away with his horse and disappeared, which was perhaps a good thing for him.

The boys had packed everything on the waggons, and were lashing the bedding in the tent-waggon so as to be out of the way of the dust and the thorns, when one of them picked up and handed out to us the open book and writing materials, just as Soltké had left them three days before, when he had jumped out to shoot the blue jay.

The diary lay open at the last-written page, and we read :

'The most verushius of reptile is the Whuy-per——'

Robbie closed the book gently and put it away. It didn't seem the least bit funny then.

At midnight, when the long night trek was over, and we were rolled in our blankets near the camp-fire, Robbie's heart was full, and he spoke—slowly and in half-broken tones :

'Ye mind the time he sent for me ? Ye do ? Yes ; well, it was to ask my forgiveness for what he said the day I struck him. Ay, he did that !'

Robbie looked slowly round the circle through dimmed glasses, and then went on hesitatingly :

'And he said, too, that we had all been too good to him, and that he had played it low on us; and that he—he hoped the good God would pardon him the greatest crime of all. And he said that I must give his Prayer-Book and his zither' (Robbie continued in a lower and reverent tone) 'to—to his child—his little boy.'

'*Soltké's child ?*' came from all together.

Robbie nodded, and there was a space of time when everyone shifted a little and felt chilled ; but it was Gowan who put our common thought into words.

' Where is his wife ?' he asked slowly.

' Dead !' said Robbie.

' I—I didn't know he was married.'

Robbie's look was a prayer for mercy, as he answered :

' He wasn't !'

INDUNA NAIRN.

I.

'MOODIE'S' was concession ground, and belonged to a company; but as 'findings is keepings' is the first law of the prospector, there were quite a number of people, otherwise honest and well-principled, who thought that it would be the right thing to rush it and peg it, and parcel it out among themselves upon such terms and conditions as a committee of their own number might decide.

So of course they rushed it !

They were good men and true, and they were strong in their righteous indignation, but in nothing else ; and when it came to trying conclusions with a Government, they, being penniless, short-rationed, and few in numbers, went under, and were carried off under arrest to Pretoria, the committee designate going in bulk, with their proposers and seconders thrown in.

It was then that the real inwardness of an em-

barrassing position was revealed. The case of
' The State *v.* H. Bankerpitt and Twenty-nine
Others' could not come on for many weeks, and
the Government, being mistrusted by the Pretoria
tradesmen, who would no longer accept 'goodfors'
of even a few shillings value, attempted to mas-
querade stern necessity as simple grace, and offered
to release the prisoners on bail.

The offer was rejected with derision.

Next day Government went one better and offered
to release them on parole without bail. But even this
did not tempt them, and eventually a delegate was
deputed to interview the prisoners so as to ascertain
their wishes. The unanimous reply was:

' You brought us here. You can keep us here.
We are quite contented.'

It was then realized that the matter was serious,
and a meeting of the Executive Council was called
and the gravity of the situation explained by the
President of the State. The result of the delibera-
tions was the presentation by the Government of
an ultimatum, which was in effect, ' Choose between
a compromise and a freeze-out.'

They accepted the compromise.

It was that the Government should find them in
lodging and they should find their board.

It was not a very grand compromise, but it was
better than a freeze-out, and during the ensuing

months in which ' The State *v.* H. Bankerpitt and
Twenty-nine Others ' sustained many adjournments
and much publicity in the Pretoria press, only once
was the *modus vivendi* thus established in any way
threatened.

The younger members of the party had begun to
keep irregular hours. One or two remonstrances
failing to effect an improvement, the worthy gaoler
resolved upon the extremest measure. He posted
the following notice on the door :

' Anyone failing to return by nine p.m. will be
locked out.'

There was no further trouble.

    *   *   *   *   *

Some months had passed since the trial. The
State had vindicated its authority ; the inherent
right of man was thrown out of court ; and ' H.
Bankerpitt and Twenty-nine Others ' had paid the
penalty for their mistaken zeal. The man in the
street had ceased to prophesy that the case would
lead to war with the suzerain power, the weekly
newspaper resumed its normal appearance, and the
' constant reader ' was no longer haunted by a
headline more constant than himself.

' Moodie's ' was controlled by its rightful owners,
but its name was as wormwood in the prospector's
mouth, and the quondam Promised Land became a
spot accursed and despised.

Across the valley of the Kaap, over the rock-crested mountains of Maconchwa, out into the shattered hills and ranges of Swazieland, and over the hot bush-hidden flats the prospectors took their ways to find something somewhere which would be their own.

They went singly and in pairs, and they 'humped swag and tucker' when they had no donkeys to pack. It was a rule with few exceptions that they only went in parties and without swag when there was a rush on.

This was one of the exceptions.

Seven men in irregular Indian file, and at irregular distances apart, were toiling up the green slopes of the Maconchwa.

They were following a path, and one after another would stop and turn panting to pay tribute to the steepness of the hill and the beauty of the view below.

Far below them, and farther still ahead, the smooth-worn path meandered over the hill's face like a red-brown thread woven in the green. The sun was fiercely strong, but the breath of the mountain was cool, and they drank it in gratefully at each rest.

They were all marked with the 'out-of-luck' brand. It was stamped on their faces. They were all tired, and most of them looked hungry as well.

When the leader reached the top, he looked expectantly around on all sides, then, stepping briskly towards an outcrop near by, from which a better view was obtainable, he looked again long and carefully. Then he came back to the path where the others had already assembled, and cursed the country and all in it from the bottom of his bitter soul.

' There's no house and there's no kraal, and there's no God-damn-nothing. It's eight hours since we started on the " two-mile " tramp, and I knew from the start we were fooled. If Choky Wilson had *known* anything he would have come himself, and not told *you*.'

He scowled at a younger member of the party who was standing by chewing a stem of grass and looking down across the Crocodile and Hlambanyati valleys.

' What did the Swazie boy say ?' asked another, turning readily on the youngster as the convenient scapegoat.

The younger one answered good-temperedly :

' He said that the White Induna was on the Maconchwa, near the first water that came out of the white rock.'

' Maconchwa !' snarled the leader, 'why, it's twenty miles long ! The whole d——d range is Maconchwa. Any idiot might be expected to know that.'

'Yes, that's why I didn't offer to explain,' said the younger one.

The thrust passed unnoticed, and while a general *indaba* was going on the last speaker moved to the same spot from which the leader had viewed the country.

He knew the Kaffir and his language and his habits, and he could read the face of the country as well as the niggers themselves, so they heeded him when he spoke, although he was the youngest member of the party, and when a few minutes later, he cut into the conversation with the remark that 'there was a cattle kraal near by and they had better go on there and ask the way,' there was a general chorus of 'Where?' and an incredulous 'Darned if I can see it!' from the leader.

The youngster replied again:

'Nor can I, but it's there all the same.'

'How do you know?'

'Look,' he said, pointing to a slope about a mile distant.

'Well, look at what?'

'Can't you see that red patch on the rise there?'

'What, those water-worn dongas?'

'Not dongas—cattle tracks. They are from the drinking-place. That must be the White Rock up there, and I expect the house must be behind the clump of trees.'

6

They walked on until the trees were reached and they could see the small rough stone house through a thinner portion of the Bush, and there they waited awhile to take counsel. It was finally decided that they should all go up together, but they looked to the one who seemed to be their leader to act as spokesman.

'If he's a white man at all,' remarked he in front, 'he won't refuse us grub, anyhow; but that's just it. They say he's no more white than old Bandine, that he hates the sight of white men, and keeps as far from them as he can. He's been so long among the darned niggers that he's just one of them himself.'

They passed along the path to the house, and six of the party waited below while the leader mounted the steps of the mud stoep.

A tall man with a long brown beard stepped out of an open doorway and met him.

The whole party offered 'good-evening' with more or less *empressement*, and certainly with a greater show of politeness than was customary with them; but the man only slid his hands easily into the pockets of a light duck-coat, and looked with critical and not too friendly glance at the leader, ignoring the others.

'We're out prospectin' about here,' began the leader, 'and we thought we'd just come along and look you up.'

As there was no reply to this, not even a
change in the look nor a twitch of a muscle to be
construed into acknowledgment of the remark,
the speaker resumed quickly and with less composure :

'The niggers told us you hung out about here,
and, bein' the only white man in these parts, we
kind o' came along to see what was doin', and if
there was any chance of reefin', and about the
licenses and water and that.'

The owner of the house continued to look
steadily and in silence at the speaker. The latter,
when the invitation of a second pause passed unac-
cepted, flushed up and, abandoning the previous
method, asked curtly :

' Can you sell us any food ? Fowls or crushed
mealies, or anything. We're half dead o' trampin'
over your d——d hills, and I want food for self
and mates. We're far down enough, but we reckon
to pay for what we get. We're not loafin' !'

The man did not appear to notice this hostile
tone any more than he had the former conciliatory
one ; but, after another deadly pause, he asked,
in a quiet, clear voice :

' Your name?'

' Bankerpitt,' said the other.

The faintest trace of a smile lit up the man's
face as he remarked quietly :

'Ah, *H.* Bankerpitt'—and glancing for the first
time at the rest of the party—'*and twenty-nine
others !*'

He turned and walked slowly into the house,
closing the door after him.

Bankerpitt had scarcely strength to say, 'Well,
I'm d——d !'

The party turned away, tired and hungry, and
marched in silence to the clump of trees near the
spruit below the house.   There was no other water
near, so they made camp for the night there.

It was dark.   Occasionally the brighter gleams
of the fire lighted up the circle of sullen faces.
There was nothing to eat or drink, so they had
settled down to a monotonous chorus of curses on
the renegade who had turned his back on his own
colour.   One by one each added his quota of bitter,
unmeasured abuse until their vocabularies, com-
prehensive as they were, began to give out, and
only now and then a mere exclamation of disgust,
or a well-brooded curse, would break the heavy
silence.

There being nothing to cook, there was nothing
to do at that time of evening but to brood on their
wrongs.   They did this thoroughly until a faint
rustle in the wood made them look round, and then
a child's voice close behind the group gave the
Kaffir salutation ' Makos !'   Someone raised a brand

from the fire, and by its light they saw two *umfaans* bearing on their, heads a large earthen bowl each. One bowl contained fresh milk, the other a stew of fowls and stamped mealies.

The boys had the look of bright intelligence characteristic of the Zulu race, but when Bankerpitt asked sharply, 'Who sent this?' they exchanged one glance, and a cloud of the densest stupidity settled on their faces. Bankerpitt repeated his question, dragging one urchin closer to the fire. The reply, given in a thin, childish treble, was:

'It is food, white man! It is here!'

'Tell me!' he said fiercely, giving the child's arm a shake, 'does it come from that white dog up there?'

Even in the urchins of the race there is the instinct of evasion which enables them to baffle the closest inquiries.

'It is food for the white man. It is here!' was all that Bankerpitt's bullying could elicit.

'If we take it, it's because we must; but, by God! we'll pay him for it, same as we would any other blasted nigger!' exclaimed Bankerpitt savagely; and he drew from his leathern beltpouch the three shillings it contained and thrust them into the *umfaan's* hand. The coins were dropped like hot coals, and the child said:

' I want no money, white man ; I bring a gift.'

But the men were hungry and took the food ;
and presently the two *umfaans* drew nearer to the
fire, and, squatting on their haunches, awaited
with ox-like patience the emptying of their bowls.
When at last the boys stood up to go, the youngest
of the party, who had been a silent and amused
witness of his leader's attempt to get information
out of them, said something in a low tone, to
which one boy replied :

' Inkosikaas.'

A soft significant whistle was the only com-
ment.

' What was that, Geddy ?' said Bankerpitt
quickly.

' I asked who sent them with the food.'

' Well, who did ?'

' He says " The missis " !'

' Shrine of the Mighty !'

*   *   *   *   *

That was the first experience of Induna
Nairn.

*   *   *   *   *

The second came this wise, about a year later.

There had been a row in Delagoa about some
cattle which had been stolen.   The rightful owners
took their own way about getting them back, for
they had more confidence in themselves than in the

Portuguese ; but, unfortunately, just at the last moment, an accident happened which made trouble for them. That was why they had been across the border away in Swazie country for so many months, and that was why they were coming back over the mountains and in a quiet way, for they were not sure of the reception which might await them.

One of them was Geddy, the youngster of the former party.

Geddy had not forgotten his experience of Nairn's 'hospitable roof,' and had given his companion, with considerable force and numerous illustrations, a fair picture of the well-remembered night. It is not surprising that they decided to give 'the d——d white nigger's ' house the ' go-by.'

Nairn's house stood on the track ; in fact, the only feasible road up the Berg was a bridle-path cut by Nairn up to his house ; thence the ordinary native paths led in all directions, and—by reason— one or more led to the Kaap. In order to pass the house in mid-trek they made their morning off-saddle below the Berg, intending by noon to be some miles beyond the Peak. Near the Berg there are two climates, one for ' below ' and one for ' on top,' and it was quite reasonable and natural to rise, as they did, out of the placid spring morning on the flats into a first-class thunderstorm with high wind and driving rain as soon as they reached the exposed plateau. The tired horses refused to face the sheets of rain, and snorted and shook with fright at the lightning stabbing here and there and everywhere, and the deafening crashes of thunder. There was nothing for it but to dismount and, as the poor brutes turned their tails to the storm, to crouch to leeward of them for such shelter as they could give, and pray to Heaven that hail would not follow the rain.

Drenched, sopping, numbed and pierced by the cold wind that succeeded the storm, they resumed their ride half an hour later. Their clothes were setting hard in the wind, their blankets—strapped over the pommels—carried pounds weight of water, and the pulpy saddles clung like indiarubber.

The poor horses toiled on, slipping and sprawling along the greasy, smooth-worn Kaffir path, and when they rounded a little koppie that flanked Nairn's house, and came suddenly on the well-worn track that led to the house itself—not twenty yards off—they pricked their ears, and with a low whinny of welcome and joy trotted towards the house. Geddy pocketed his pride and, bowing to circumstances that were too much for him, allowed his horse to follow the other's lead. He did not, however, dismount as the other did, but sat in the saddle with an air of neutrality, awaiting the turn of events.

Geddy was prepared for many possible develop-
ments, and—by reason of the feeling description
given him of the previous visit—his companion
was also forearmed against contingencies, and was
ready with replies suited to any form of incivility;
but when Nairn stepped out on to the stoep looking
infinitely amused, and remarked frankly, 'By Gad!
you are two miserable-looking objects !'—when
this happened the two just looked down at themselves and then at each other, and finally burst into
laughter more genuine and prolonged than the
ostensible cause would seem to warrant.

The house must have contained four rooms ; but
they only saw two. It was a very quiet place.
Oddly enough there were no dogs about, and the
fowls did not seem to be as self-assertive there as
Swazie fowls usually are. There were no noises at
all about the place, not even the welcome sounds of
life. All seemed to be toned down, *weighed* down,
to about the level of sociability which had marked
Nairn's manner on the first visit. Geddy, feeling
a little mean, it is true, was careful not to betray
any indications of having been there before, but
while they were getting into dry clothing in Nairn's
bedroom, he drew his companion's attention to a
large calabash that stood on the window-sill half
full of milk. It had been cracked, and there was a
small V-shaped nick in the rim, below which, and

encircling the gourd itself, was a delicate network
of plaited brass, copper, and iron wires.

'That was the one the milk came in that night,'
said Geddy, in a whisper. 'I remember spilling
some on account of that nick, and then I noticed
the wire.'

His companion nodded. It was not an important nor even a very interesting discovery.

The younger waited a little, and then, slightly
disgusted at the other's slowness, said :

'Well, either he sent the grub to us himself,
or——'

'Or what ?'

'Or—— Where's the missis ?'

They took in the room at a glance ; but there
was no answering evidence there. And when they
joined Nairn they found that there were easy-chairs
in the dining-room ; so there they sat and smoked,
and watched the rain set in as the regular spring
drizzle does above the Berg.

The chairs, like the rest of the furniture, were
rough-made from bushwood ; but it seemed odd
that a hermit should have three. There was a
bookcase in the room, and it was full of well-
bound and well-worn books, 'mostly odd volumes—
very few series,' as Geddy remarked afterwards.
There were a good many books of science, and all
the poets he could recall ; and there were books in

Latin, French, Greek, and German. Somehow he did not like to ask the real questions he wanted to put about the books. He did not quite know how far to go. In reply to one question, Nairn had said dryly that he had brought them with him, and was apparently indisposed to say more. He was not an easy man to draw.

During the day they had evidence of the respect in which Nairn was held by his dependents. He spoke to them in the lowest possible voice and in the fewest possible words, and never—except once, when something had occurred which annoyed him—never looked at, or even in the direction of, the individual addressed. On that occasion he was asking a question of a tall and remarkably good-looking Swazie woman.

She stood like a bronze statue while he spoke, and when he looked at her and his eyes blazed anger, although his voice did not alter, the colour rose to the woman's face, and turned her brown skin a reddish-bronze. Her head was slowly lowered, and 'the only answer was a faint whisper of the word, 'Inkos—chief!' The incident was trifling, but Geddy noticed it, and noted that his way with his boys and the men about the place was the same, and began to see why they called him 'Induna Nairn.'

As the rain had not abated Nairn insisted upon

their remaining overnight. He was pleasant, courteous, and most interesting, full of the strangest and most intimate knowledge of the country and the natives. He frequently illustrated remarks by references to other countries and other people, but neither of his guests cared to put the direct question as to whether he had been to those countries or only read of them. He gave no information about himself. Geddy was not satisfied with this, and with his sense of what is due to one's host somewhat dulled—doubtless by the recollection of his previous visit—took every opportunity of leading up to those topics which Nairn most avoided, but which Geddy hoped would throw a light upon the man himself.

Beaten on the subject of the books, baffled when he led up to personal experiences, foiled gently but firmly at every attempt, Geddy at last got an inspiration and laid for a bold stroke.

They were at dinner, and the peculiarly savoury character of the stew recalled to the youngster again the question that had been puzzling him all along. Summoning all his nerve, he said with cheery zest:

' By Jove, Nairn, after months of roast mealies and tough game—without salt, too—this does taste delicious !'

' Glad you like it,' said his host quietly. ' Staple

dish, you know. Just stewed fowl and stamped mealies !'

' Yes, by George ! but such a stew ! Who— who's your cook ?'

' Well, I suppose it becomes an easy task when the bill of fare doesn't vary once a month ;' and Nairn looked up curiously at his guest.

' But how do you manage it, eh ? No boy ever cooked like this.'

Nairn delayed replying until a faint guilty flush touched up the other's cheeks, and then laughingly—and with a significant look of complete intelligence—he said :

' I was just wondering, Mr. Geddy, if you were as favourably impressed with it *the last time you were here ?'*

Had the roof dropped in on him the collapse of Geddy would not have been more complete. Heron laughed unrestrainedly, perhaps because (as has been said) there is something not altogether dis-pleasing in the misfortunes of our friends ; perhaps, too, because his view of the incident referred to was untinged by the bitter sense of personal humili-ation, and his humour had therefore full play.

Nairn did not press his discomfited guest, but, smiling pleasantly, took up the burden of the talk.

'I know quite well what you thought of me, and I know even something of what you said about "the white dog," etc., but I think (and I fancy neither of you will take offence at plain speaking)—I think that I did right in repulsing what had all the appearance of imposition.' He pushed back his chair and turned to the younger man. ' Just put yourself in my place, now, Geddy. I came to this place of my own choice. I seek nothing of other men, and I desire to go my own way unmolested. I was here before your people came in their feverish hunt for gold. I dare say I shall be here when you have ended the fruitless search. If things should turn against me and your luck be in the ascendant—why! there is room in Africa for us both. I can move on.'

Nairn spoke in an easy, unemotional way, as though discussing an abstract question of minor importance.

'Do you know,' he continued after a while, 'I sought out this spot and I chose this life because here there is no nineteenth century, no struggle, no ambition, no unrest. Here is absolute peace and content for me because I need take no thought of the morrow. You who spend your lives and energies on the outside edge of civilization paving a way for others' feet—you are beglamoured by your "life of freedom, adventure, and romance." My dear sirs, that is a view that I cannot pretend even to understand, much less sympathize with.

It may appear unnatural to you, but it is a fact, that I dislike the society of civilized men, and most of all that of the pioneers—the sappers and miners of civilization—who think a white skin a warrant for anything. Odd as it may seem to you, *I* do not regard each white man as a friend or a brother. On the contrary, I see in him a possible enemy and a certain nuisance.'

Nairn leaned back in his chair, and thoughtfully polished the bowl of his pipe.

They had finished dinner, and were lighting up for a smoke. The others puffed away in silence.

He had said his say candidly and without heat, and no offence had been meant or taken. Presently Heron said:

'What puzzles me, Nairn, is, since you distrust every white man you see, what the devil made you ask *us* in?'

'Aye! that's it,' said Geddy good-humouredly. 'That's the very question I was going to ask. What made you change your opinion?'

'Well,' said Nairn, with simple directness, 'your case is peculiar. I had a certain sympathy with you, you see, for we are all outlaws together—I from choice!'

Both men coloured faintly, and Geddy asked at once:

'How could you know that at the time? How did you know us—or me?'

'My dear fellow, I knew you by several means. In the first place, I had met you before—you see, I do not see so many white faces that I can't remember them ; and in the second place, the *umfaan* to whom you spoke that night, you recollect, also recognised you.'

Geddy, who recalled in a flash both the question he had asked that night and the answer given by the boy, shrank under Nairn's direct, calm look.

'But,' he continued without pause, 'you forget —or did you not know?—that for a month there was a detachment of police on the watch for you here.'

'Lucifer! What luck we didn't come sooner !' exclaimed Heron, aghast. 'They'd have had us, as sure as God made little apples !'

'Oh, that was all right,' said Nairn, smiling. 'I was well posted as to their plans and movements. You see, I heard of your affair in Delagoa, and I knew you had gone for a spell to Mahaash's and Sebougwaan's, and you were safe enough there. In any case, I took the precaution of sending word to Mahaash to stop you if you wanted to come back before the coast was clear. He had a letter for you from me for some time, but returned it yesterday with a message to say you were coming this way, and that was why I was expecting you when you turned up this morning.'

Geddy put out his hand, saying :

' By God, Nairn, you are a trump ! You've been a perfect Providence to us ; and—and I take back all I said about you that other time.'

Nairn smiled and shook his head.

' I'm afraid,' he answered, ' that it was only because you were in a scrape that I sided with you at all. It seemed a bit of a d——d shame that the Government should set on a couple of fellows because they had chosen to settle their grievances their own way, which is what you did, I believe?'

Heron smiled grimly, and nodded reply.

' You seem to have had pretty good information about us,' Geddy remarked. ' I suppose your neighbours keep you well posted ?'

' Yes ; there are Boswells among them, too. I have had faithfully retailed to me the whole of the affair of Mahaash and the silver spur. Don't put another chief to ride a bucking horse with a spur. They may not all fall as lightly as Mahaash, and they may not all be as good-tempered.'

' Upon my soul,' said Heron, ' I did it in perfect good faith. He wanted a present, and I gave him what I could best spare. How could I possibly know that that old crock would buck ?'

' Well, you had a lucky escape. Umketch

7

would have had you kerried. They don't like to
appear ridiculous. How did you lose your pocket-
book, Geddy ?'
' How—the—deuce——'
Nairn laughed heartily.
' Why, man, it has been here for weeks, waiting
for you! They bring me all these things, with
their gossip and their troubles. An old fellow, a
witch-doctor, brought the pocket-book. He said
he found it by divination—casting the dollas ; the
old fraud! He walked up here, some forty miles,
just to gossip about you. It took him three days
before he produced the book. The first day he
talked of the prospects of rain, and the grass and
the cattle ; the next he spoke about the rumours
that were afloat about white men working into the
ground and bursting it open with guns, and
wondered if white men would overrun Swazieland;
and he wound up with the admission that he had
heard of two having been seen, and on horseback,
too, and with rifles. Notwithstanding which, he
believed them to be English, for one had given a
shilling to a young girl as a present, and the other
had a book in which he wrote. There it is on the
shelf beside you. He wanted to sell it, but I took
it from him, and told him he would probably have
bad luck, and one of his cows would be barren
or lose her calf this year because he had meddled

with your goods, and failed to return the book to you. He stole it, of course ?'

' The old scoundrel !' said Geddy, reaching for the book ; ' he must have found it while we were yet in sight. I left it in a hut in one of the kraals.'

' Yes ; I'm afraid he was an old thief,' said Nairn. ' The raw Swazie would think nothing of a twenty or thirty mile jaunt to return it ; but these witch-doctors are mostly old Basuto ruffians, steeped in guile. They have few scruples when there is a prospect of profit.'

' On my word,' laughed Heron, ' I don't know what you may not know about us with agencies like this, and a whole nation making a confidante of you ! What a rum life you do lead !'

Nairn looked at him curiously, and remarking dryly that they were a very peculiar people, rose from his seat, and made it clear that he thought it time for bed. He showed them to his own room, where an extra bed had been fixed up, and wishing them ' Good-night,' left them.

Quoth Geddy :

' I didn't like to ask him where he would sleep if we took his room, as one feels bound to do in common civility. I'd have got another of those gentle cold-blooded sneers for my pains. You know, old chap, with all due respect—and all that sort of thing—for our host, he's beastly uncivil the moment you ask questions. It's a regular case of scratch the Russian and you find the Tartar.'

'Yes; you're right. Although it seems a bit ungrateful to say so, I'm dashed if I'd care to have much to do with him. Did you see him shut up when I remarked about his living a queer life? Gad! his lips closed up until they fitted like the valves of an oyster. He's as suspicious as the devil!'

'I say, look here—a photo! Just look, man! " Harrison Nairn" on the back of it! Quite a decent-looking chap. Heron, I wonder who *she* is?'

'God knows! I don't!'

'Someone else's, you can bet, or he wouldn't lie so low, eh?'

'H'm! looks devilish like it.'

'I say, Heron.'

'What?'

'I wonder what he'd say if he heard us, eh?'

'Shut up, man; go to sleep!'

'I say! The ideal white man—" a possible enemy and a certain nuisance."'

'For Heaven's sake, man, shut up! They'll hear you sniggering. Good-night!'

II.

It was a dark night and still—the stillness that often precedes a thunderstorm. The clouds were banked up thick, and only here and there on the outer fringes, where cuts in the hills gave a glimpse nearer the horizon, was there a faint lighting of the gloomy canopy.

Low's Creek runs through one of Nature's perfect amphitheatres and finds its outlet at the Poort. If that were blocked, there would be a lake many hundred feet deep; but as it is not blocked, there is only a very clear, sparkling stream rippling over stony bottoms, or swirling under the overhanging thorns and fig-trees—the one constant babbler on such nights as this. The road through this valley is not over-good at the best of times, and it is something worse than bad on a really dark night— which was exactly what the driver of the spider- and-four thought as he pulled up with his near fore-wheel foul of a dead tree-stump. There was no damage done, for the horses were pleased to take the sudden check as an excuse, if not indeed a hint, to stop; and when by the light of matches the size of the obstacle was determined, and means were found to free the wheel, the driver said, 'Come!' and the horses toiled on again up the hill towards the Neck. Every now and then, as they climbed

slowly up, the ladies—there were two ladies in
the spider—would point out the camp-fires of the
prospectors at various heights and distances on the
tops or slopes of the surrounding hills, and their
companion would tell them which was French
Bob's, and which the Cascade, and point out, high
and far, the famous Kimberley Imperial; and the
Hottentot driver would peer out in front, silently
intent upon the road.

Toiling, swaying, and straining, they at last
reached the Neck, and gave the horses a blow.
Behind them, or rather below them, black as the
bottomless pit, lay the valley out of which they had
risen. In front lay the broader, shallower, furrowed
basin, through which the road winds, cross-cut by
Honeybird and Fig-tree Creeks; and beyond Avoca,
where the waters meet, they could see, through the
gap of the Queen's River Poort, the lightning playing in the distance—silent, clear, and not too vivid.

Down the easy slope the horses trotted out freely,
swinging their heads and snorting as the faint, cool
breeze, the sure precursor of the storm, fanned and
freshened them. On they went gaily for a couple
of miles till the deep, dry donga was reached, where
the road dips down suddenly into a black, murky,
impenetrable darkness. Above, the trees on either
side of the high banks intertwine their branches;
beneath, the soft dead leaves lie upon a sandy bottom,

and the road is flanked by jungle, pure and simple.
It is like a tunnel. It is not possible to leave it
except at the ends.

The driver gave the leaders their heads, and
trusted to their knowing that he couldn't see, whilst
they might. The heavy grating of the brake, hard
pressed, sounded loud on the night air as the leaders
disappeared into the dark trough. Down went the
trap and horses with a diver's plunge at first, and
then more steadily and slowly they neared the
bottom ; but before it was reached, the leaders shied
violently to the off, the spider swung down the
slope, slid a little, poised for a moment on two
wheels, and turned slowly over on its side on the
bed of leaves and sand. The horses, with their
heads jammed in the bush, were effectually stopped.

The ladies did not scream!

It seems wrong—unnatural; but they did not.
Urgent need and sudden danger, as they overwhelm
and stupefy some, so do they brace and brighten
others ; and when one of the horses whinnied in a
friendly way, it seemed odd that it should be a
girl's voice that exclaimed quickly:

'Listen! they're not frightened. It must be
another horse!'

'Are you hurt?' 'Where are you?' and, 'Are
you all right?' were exchanged in the darkness ; and
then someone struck a match, and, making a dark

lantern of his hat, threw the light on the late occupants of the spider.

The girls were dusty, pale, and frightened, and the men looked anxious. The Hottentot driver was swearing to himself in a discontented undertone, and endeavouring concurrently to loosen the wheelers' harness.

'I am the culprit,' said the man with the light. 'I can only say I am very delighted that no one is hurt, and awfully sorry that I gave you such a fright. I'm sure I never meant it. I did not know there was a soul within miles until the sound of your brake frightened my horse into backing into the bush here. The brute wouldn't budge, so I sat still, hoping that you would pass without seeing me.'

'Oh, it really doesn't matter in the least!' came from one of the girls, as the match died out. 'You don't know how relieved, how grateful we are to you for not being a lion or a highwayman.'

The driver Piet had rummaged out a stump of candle, and lighted it. It flickered uncertainly on the capsized spider, on the scattered cushions and shawls, on the faces of the two young girls and their companion, and faintly lighted up the lank form and the dark bearded face of the enemy.

'I thought I knew your voice, Heron!' said the latter quietly.

'Nairn! By all that's great and wonderful! What on earth were you——'

'Well, I wasn't waylaying you with evil intent, and I do hope that the ladies——'

'Oh, I forgot. My sisters,' said Heron, with an explanatory wave. 'Girls, this is Mr. Nairn, a friend of mine. Very much in disguise, you must admit, Nairn!'

'Indeed I do. I confess, I repent, and I beg for mercy; and, to give practical proof of my sincerity, let me help you. Come on, Heron ; let's right the trap first.'

No damage had been done to the trap, and the three men soon succeeded in getting it on its wheels again. The boy drove through the donga and up the other bank without further difficulty, the others preferring to walk ; but out there, when he had room to move round his team, the driver found that the off-leader had gashed his shoulder badly in the bush, and would have to be turned out.

Heron's heart sank, for it would be a serious matter to attempt the four drifts of the Queen's River in a heavy spider with only a pair. He looked at the overcast sky, and turned in despair to Nairn, who had remained with the ladies, and knew nothing of the injury to the horse.

'Nairn, you know the road best. Is there *any* place where we can stay the night ? We can't tackle the rivers. One of the leaders has cut his shoulder badly and won't face the harness. We must put up somewhere for the night!'

'There's Clothier's,' the other answered; 'but I'm afraid that won't do—a grass hut, and sardines, gin, and rough customers. Charlie Brandt's— ditto! There's the Queen of Sheba's at Eureka City; but, then, you'd never reach there alive— at night. Let's see! No; there's no fit place between this and Barberton.'

'There!' said Heron, 'we'll spend a pleasant night in the veld, rain and all. I wish we'd come on a bit further with the waggons. It will be rough on you girls.'

But they did not seem dismayed at the prospect; in fact, they considered it a romantic sort of picnic adventure. Heron, who had had malarial fever, took no count of the romance.

While the matter was being discussed, Nairn went forward and carefully examined the injured horse. Heron had decided to outspan where they were, under a big Dingaan apricot-tree, and the ladies were busy making plans for the disposal of cushions, wraps, and rugs to fend off the coming rain.

'That horse will be worse to-morrow than he is to-night. He won't be well for weeks,' said Nairn coolly. 'How do you propose getting on at all, even if you do stay here to-night? What do you gain by the delay?'

Heron was somewhat taken aback.

'Well,' he answered, 'we gain the daylight, anyway; that's something.'

'Something—yes; but daylight won't take you through the rivers with one pair of horses. They'll be pretty full, too, after to-night's rain.'

'That's true,' said Heron gloomily; 'and it's raining like old Harry now up at the headwaters. Look at the lightning over the Kaap Valley!'

They looked, and the quick play of the distant flashes left no room for doubt. Then Nairn spoke again—without impulse, without enthusiasm, but deliberately, as though he had considered the matter and reluctantly but finally made his decision.

'You will have to put my horse in place of the injured one, and go on to-night. I can walk.'

He did not affect that the idea was the happy thought of the moment, or that it was from all points of view a good one. He seemed from his tone to be making the best of a bad job, and Heron saw that so distinctly that he could only stammer out weakly:

'Oh, really, it's awfully good of you, but we couldn't allow you to walk.'

But the taller of the two girls came to her brother's assistance.

' I think it's a *capital* idea! Don't you see, Jack, Mr. Nairn wants "to give a practical proof of his sincerity"?'

The lazy, mischievous imitation of Nairn's tone and manner in quoting his own words brought a hearty laugh from the others against Nairn, for he had 'given himself away'; and once or twice as they were changing horses and preparing to start, Nairn found himself looking curiously at the girl who had 'let him down.'

They were nearly ready to start when she came over to him, and said :

'You are not going to walk. You will come with us, won't you?'

He shook his head.

'My way is not your way, Miss Heron.'

'No, no ; you express it wrongly. *My* way is *your* way. We have room for you and you must come.'

'But I have just come from Barberton, and I live in—in the Swazie country.' And his voice dropped to nothing on the last words.

'Now, Mr. Nairn, I know you are afraid of over-crowding us. You *have* to come for your horse, so that excuse won't do ; and since you compel me to tell the whole truth, Jack says you know the road best, and we want you to come because we are just a tiny little bit afraid of those horrid rivers. Now I've told you.'

Nairn submitted ; but as they drove along in the dark more than once the thought occurred that even the best of women will stoop to the most unfair means to gain their points.

After many years it was all fresh to him again.

They spun along the smooth soft road, slowing up in places for the dongas—those deeply-worn furrows in Nature's face, the result of many a heavy storm. They passed the huge old fig-tree standing sentinel where the waters meet, and crossed the Fig-tree Creek, which, to the experienced ear of the men, had a fuller and angrier tone than was its wont. They passed 'Clothier's' in silence. To the girls the grass shanty leaking candle-light at every pore in its misshapen sides, the shouts of laughter, the half-heard songs, the glimpse of the interior as they passed the door, showing the rough gin-case counter, backed by shelves laden with 'square face,' and the bare-armed, bearded man craning over to dodge the glare of guttering candles and see who or what was passing by—all made a picture unique and indelible.

They wound slowly round the bend and over the big smooth rocks down to the Fourth Drift.

The water ran silently over the sandy bottom, and when the horses were in breast-high and their movements no longer caused a splash, the absolute stillness begat a feeling of awe and fear of the black-looking water that is so silent, so strong, and so treacherous.

To everyone there comes a sense of strain relieved and spirits reviving on coming through a bad river, and to the young girls, whose first experience it was, the splashing of the leaders' feet in shallow water, and the rising up the sandy bank, brought an ecstasy of relief.

Driving up the valley of the Lampogwana, Nairn and Heron cheered them with tales of the goldfields and of the country, and ignored the river and the coming storm; but the steep rush into the Third Drift, and the tossing and jolting over the boulders, and the angry racing of the water and the more distinct roll of the thunder, were features in a first experience which were not to be talked away, and if Nairn felt his conversational powers disparaged by very evident non-attention, perhaps this was compensated for by occasional graspings of his arm—mute appeals for protection which men take as compliments.

Going slowly down the cutting to the Second Drift, the course of the river was shown up by the lightning, and one bluish gleam in particular lit up the scene with such unsurpassable vividness that long after all was black again the eye retained a view of dark water in swirls and curves of wonderful grace, of foam-crested breakers and jets of spray, of swaying shrubs and bent, quivering reeds.

Nairn recalled another such night when his horse, which had paused to sniff before facing the flood, jerked his head up with a snort as a blinding flash had shown him a white face for an instant above the water. The fixed stare that the dead eyes gave him lingered long after succeeding flashes had shown an unbroken surface of river again. But he did not speak of this.

They drove slowly over the little flat through which the river ran, and as that was barely covered by the flood they knew that the river was just passable for the spider, but it meant getting a wetting as it was dangerously near flood mark.

Piet pulled up. The ladies and the baases, he said, could take the footpath along the mountains over the krantzes and avoid the two drifts. It was only four miles to the next hotel. He would like to outspan and stay where he was—the river was too full, and the next drift would be worse still. The river was coming down.

But Heron was obstinate, and Nairn, who knew the footpath past the Golden Valley, knew it to be an impossible alternative for ladies, at night; so Heron called out: 'Kate, you grip the rail, and Nairn will look after you! You hang on to me, Nell!' They went in, and the water washed on to

the seats, and the spider swayed to the stream ; but
the horses headed up bravely, and buoying on the
waters, or sousing underneath, half swimming and
half wading, they pulled through.

'Hold up, Nell! hold up, little woman! Don't
cry now, we're as safe as houses !' was what Nairn
heard from the opposite seat.

What happened beside him was that his companion's grasp loosened on the rail, and as the
spider rose up the soft, sandy bank, she slid back
against him with her weight on the arm he had
passed behind her as protection, and her cheek
against his shoulder.

When they pulled up on the level road again,
while her sister was laughing off her tears, Kate
pulled herself together with an effort, and said,
with a half-sobbing laugh :

'I was very fri—frightened that time. I—I
think I should have fallen out but for you.'

Then the storm broke over them, and the rain
came down in blinding torrents, and the horses,
ducking and swaying before it, moved slowly on.
Flash after flash lit up the hills above and the river
below as they toiled along where the road was cut
out of the precipitous hillside. Every furrow was
a stream, every gutter a watercourse ; the water
seemed to gush from the very earth ; the river
itself was a seething mud-red torrent.

The First Drift, which, as they were coming up stream, was their last, is broader, and not as deep as the others ; but in those days it was full of boulders, and the water raced down in three separate channels, although the surface showed but one broad stream. The drift is now higher up, where the bed is even, and the current is not so strong. They have also a wire rope across, and a ferry-boat ; but it was not so in '87. They have done a good deal to improve things, but still the river is king, and asserts itself upon occasion ; as when it took a thousand tons of solid masonry from the Cerro de Pasco dam a hundred yards below this drift, and carried samples of dressed stone and Portland cement to the barbel and crocodiles of Ingwenye Umkulu, thirty miles away ; or when, later still, it rose in protest against the impudence of man, and swept battery houses off like corks, and flung the huge girders of the railway-bridge from its path, and tossed fifty-ton boulders like pebbles into the Oriental water-race, seventy feet above the river's bed.

They crossed the first channel safely ; and they even got through the second and worst. The little Hottentot Piet sat tight, and handled his team with the most perfect skill. At times it seemed impossible that horses or trap could with-

8

stand the surging mass of water that piled up against them ; but they did. A cheering word or a timely touch of the whip seemed once or twice to avert catastrophe.

Nairn's horse had made a perfect leader, and faced the water like a steamboat ; but the other seemed to be losing heart, and but for Piet's whip would have headed down stream in the second channel.

They were into the third channel, and were going slowly and steadily through, when one front wheel came block up against a boulder, and the near leader again headed down. Whip, voice and rein failed, and as Piet made one more determined effort, something gave, and he dropped back in his seat, calling out :

' Baas, baas, the rein's broken !'

Nairn jumped up instantly, but the frightened girl clung to him, crying out :

' Oh, don't leave me ! Mr. Nairn, for the love of God, don't leave us !'

Her one hand grasped the collar of his coat, the other held his right hand. He loosened her grasp, and holding both her hands tightly, forced her back into the seat.

' Hold *that!*' he said, placing her one hand on the rail, and stooping until his face almost touched hers. ' Sit still, and wait for me. I won't desert you !'

Vaulting over into the driver's seat, he seized the sjambok and jumped into the river. The near leader, free of the check of the rein, was giving before the stream, and had turned fairly down the river. Nairn was swept off his feet in an instant, but, anticipating this, he had grasped the wheeler's near trace, and was able to work his way forward until he was abreast of the swerving leader. Keeping with his right hand a firm grasp of the lower trace, he shouted to the quaking animal, and struck it sharply on the neck and jaw with the sjambok. The suddenness of the attack startled the horse, and he plunged up stream again. At the same moment Piet's whip whistled overhead, and his voice rang out ; the other three horses strained together, and the spider rose over the stone, and, lurching and bumping, came through the third channel.

The excited animals rushed the last narrow strip of water, and Nairn, stumbling over rocks as best he could, was dragged with them, until, losing his hold and his footing with the last plunge of the horses, he was hurled forward on his head as they reached the bank. One of the horses trampled him, and two of the wheels went over his chest. The little Hottentot saw it all, and before the others knew anything, he had jumped off, leaving the horses to pull up as they were accustomed to on

8—2

the bank, and grabbed Nairn by the arm just as he began to swing into the current and float down stream.

    *   *   *   *   *

The Bungalow was perched on the hillside, and overlooked the camp. The thatched roof and wide veranda made it cool and pleasant, and the view across the great valley of De Kaap was grand.

Nairn's head was still bandaged, and he was propped up on a cushioned lounge, unable to stir.

The French window of the room opened out upon the stoep, and from the couch itself Nairn could overlook the camp and see the bold parapets of the Devil's Kantoor five-and-twenty miles across the valley.

Nairn moved his head slowly and painfully as he heard a light footstep upon the stoep. Miss Heron walked in with a cup of something in one hand, and with the other grasping the folds of her riding-habit.

'Well, how is the head?' she asked, putting down the cup and busying herself at once, fixing the cushions more comfortably, and moistening the lint and bandage over his temples. 'Better, aren't you? See, I've brought you something cool and nice to drink. It will freshen you up again. Try some!'

Nairn closed his eyes, and half turned his head away, ignoring the offer.

'You are going out again, riding?' he queried, in an uncivil tone.

'Yes; as far as the river, to see how it looks in daylight, and in its better mood. They say it is beginning to fall; but it is banks over still. They say that the morning after we crossed, Welsh, whose house is on the rise above the drift, got out of bed into two feet of water. He says he felt it in bed, but thought it was only the roof leaking again. I wish you could come with us—but you will soon, won't you?'

'No; I've stayed too long already,' was the surly answer, and Nairn turned his face further towards the wall.

'To-morrow we shall be able to move you out on to the stoep, and perhaps you will let me read to you there? It won't seem so lonely and dismal then,' said Miss Kate, gently ignoring Nairn's tone.

'Thank you!' he answered tartly; 'I don't mind being alone. I like it!'

She had got to know his humours, and so, standing back a little where he could not watch her face, and keeping the laughter out of her voice, she said: 'Oh!'

'Perhaps the others are ready,' he remarked after a pause. 'I am keeping you from your ride.'

'I don't think so. They promised to call for me here.'

'Don't wait on my account, please. I don't mind being alone.'

'So you said before. If you *object* to my sitting here, of course I can wait on the stoep. I thought perhaps you liked me to be here.'

Miss Kate switched gently at her foot, but did not move from her seat, and Nairn played a tattoo upon the woodwork of the lounge. He broke the silence with an impatient sigh and, after another pause, his companion remarked airily to the opposite wall:

'I wonder why sick people are called *patients?*'

Nairn twitched visibly, but offered no explanation, and there was another silence. Presently the girl observed genially:

'You remember, Mr. Nairn, while we were driving along that night, you were telling us about the training of horses? You remember, don't you?'

'Yes,' said Nairn grumpily.

'You remember,' resumed the girl, smiling sweetly—'you remember telling us that you considered the various types of animals higher or lower according to their susceptibility to kindness and gentle treatment—that the horse, for instance, stands higher than the mule or the donkey. Now,' said she, turning to him with laughing eyes but earnest mien, 'I wanted to ask you which of those two is the one upon which patience and kindness and good temper are most wasted.'

'You mean, whether I am a mule or an ass ?'

Nairn looked round, vainly endeavouring not to smile.

'Oh dear, oh dear !' said Miss Kate, laughing and moving to the door ; 'I'm afraid the poor old head is very bad to-day ! Here are the others. I must go. Good-bye.'

'*Did* you mean that *I*——'

'Say good-bye at once, or I'll sit down again and refuse to leave.'

'I won't ! Tell me, did——'

'Good-bye, Ursa Major with the sore head, and don't ask questions.'

The girl curtseyed to him in the doorway as she left, and Nairn turned his face to the wall again with a groan.

A girl knows when a man's eyes follow her about the room, and she knows why—long before the man does. But the man finds it out soon enough.

Nairn pushed away the books and papers. They had no charm for him, and, as he could not sleep, he fell presently to tracing the design of the wall-paper and counting how many varieties or bunches of flowers went to make up the general pattern.

He detected small irregularities in the joinings, and they annoyed him. So he turned round and stared at the ceiling; but he had studied that before, and he knew which board contained the most knots, and how many boards had apparently been cut from the same log. There were two boards which were twins; so exactly did they match, they must have been parted by but one saw-cut; and he speculated if there could be any sort of intelligence in them that could be roused to wonder or gratitude that they, cut in Norway from one stately old pine, should pass through many hands and yet find a resting-place side by side ten thousand miles away in the gold-fields of the Transvaal.

Nairn's eyelids drooped heavily. One sleepy chuckle escaped him at his own quaint conceit, as he wondered whether the ceiling boards considered the flooring boards beneath them, and if they ever put on side on that account; and the smile of lazy content remained long after he was fast asleep.

It was the scent of flowers that roused him. Violets! And he had not smelt them for twelve years!

Miss Kate was sitting there looking at him, and, but for the scent of the flowers and the slanting sunbeams, he might have thought she had never left.

' Does the big bear like flowers ?'

He was too contented to do more than smile.

'And he won't eat me now ?'

'When Beauty picked the flowers, what did the Beast do ?'

Kate looked up with a shade of alarm. She was not quite sure where analogies might lead them—they get to mean so much.

'Well, well,' she laughed, 'who would have suspected you of a leaning towards fairy tales ? Why don't you ask if I enjoyed my ride ?'

'Well, did you ?'

'Listen to him ! Well, *did* I ? Oh,' said Miss Kate, pushing back her chair with a sigh of mock despair, ' you'll *never* learn ! It is not in you to be ordinarily civil. Now listen, and I'll teach you ; and now repeat after me : " I hope——" '

' I hope——'

' No, no ! You must hope with greater warmth. Say, " I *hope* you have enjoyed——" '

' I *hope* you have enjoyed——'

' " Your ride *immensely !*" '

' Your ride *immensely !*'

' That's better. " And I'm very glad indeed——" '

' And I'm very glad indeed——'

' " That you went out." '

' No, I'm hanged if I'll say that !'

' Mister Nairn !'

'No ; I don't care what you say ! I won't say that ! I'm not going to perjure myself.'

' You must say it!'

' Not if I die for it !'

' You won't say it to oblige me ?'

' N—no.'

There was a curious pause. Kate looked down, saying softly :

' Well, if you won't do the first thing I have ever asked you, I suppose I'd better go.'

Women, not excepting the very best, are often most unfair, and sometimes even mean. Why change in a breath from chaff to deadly earnest, and wring a man's heart out with half a look and a catch in the voice ? Nairn succumbed.

' No, don't go. I'll say it.'

' Well ?'

' But I've forgotten the words.'

' No ; you can't have forgotten so quickly. Say, " I'm very glad indeed that you went out." '

' I'm very glad indeed that——'

'Go on !'

' That—that you've come back.'

' I can see that you want to drive me away.'

' No, don't—don't go ! " That you went out." Heaven forgive me ! There, are you satisfied ?'

' Yes, I'm satisfied now. I hate to give in—especially to a man.'

' And to a woman ?'

' Oh, I never give in to a woman. Women are so obstinate, and they're always wrong ! What are you laughing at ? Oh, well, I'm not like a woman now. I'm—you know what I mean—I'm stating the case. Besides, I meant *other* women.'

' Now, if I tell you something, you won't laugh at me and point the finger of scorn and press the heel of triumph ?'

' No, I won't.'

' Promise.'

' I promise.'

' Well, then, I *am* glad that you went out, and I *was* a bear to grudge it to you. And you—you have been far too good to me—far too good.'

' No, no—indeed no ! You are my charge, and I am your nurse. And, remember, had it not been for us you would not have been hurt. Had it not been for you we should not have been here. We brought you to death's door, and you saved us. I —I was only teasing you. I never meant——'

' Kate, child, Kate !'

' Hush ! No, no—not now. Here is George. Good-night.'

* * * * *

Yes, truly ! The—man—finds—it—out—soon —enough !

* * * * *

In the morning Nairn and his horse were gone,
and there was not a vestige of a trace to show
how, why, or where! It was several days later that
Geddy, who had been away for some weeks, dined
at Heron's, and, as they were sitting on the stoep
smoking and chatting, remarked :

'By the way, fancy whom I met on the way in !
Our old friend Induna Nairn, looking ghastly, poor
devil! Said he'd had a spill crossing a river or
something. Surlier than ever. Glared at me with
positive hatred when I asked him where he was
going to to escape civilization, and said, "Zambesi,
or hell." I could make nothing of him. Can't
stand chaff, you know ; never could. But I heard
all about him from old Tom Callan—"Hot Tom,"
you know.'

Heron looked up curiously, but did not interrupt.

'It seems he's quite a great gun among the
niggers—a real Induna. Did you know that ? I
thought it was only a nickname, but it isn't. He's
a sort of relation of the king's, etc.'

'What the devil are you talking about ?'

'Eh ? what ? A—a relation of the king's, I
said.'

'A *relation !* Nairn ?'

'Well, a connection. You know what I mean.
He married the king's favourite daughter.'

'Great God !'

'Yes. You see, we were quite on the wrong tack. By George! I did laugh when I heard it.'

Heron walked out on to the gravel path for a breath of air—out to ease the choking feeling in his throat; and he saw his sister rise from her chair, draw a shawl over her head, and move away to her own room.

That night there had come to the house a little Swazie boy. He had one very miserable fowl for sale, and he squatted on his haunches near the gate, heedless of the fact that his offer had been twice refused. Through the night he stayed, and into the morning, and as the hot sun swung overhead he sat and waited still, never taking his eyes off the front stoep. And when at last Kate came out he tried his luck again.

She turned her armchair so as to get a good light on her book, and began to read, but in a few moments the child's voice close by startled her. She looked up and saw a little black face, lighted by bright eyes and a flash of white teeth; in front of that, a wretched fowl lying on the cement stoep; and in front of that again, a folded note bearing her name. She picked up the note and read it.

'I had forgotten what a good woman was. Heaven bless you, Kate! It is not that I am ungrateful, but I wish to God Piet had left me to the river.'

Kate leaned back quietly in the Madeira armchair, and closed her eyes. When she looked again the little *umfaan* was gone ; but he had forgotten his fowl upon the stoep, which was an unusual thing for any *umfaan* to do.

CASSIDY.

'And the greatest of these is charity.'

I MET Cassidy under trying circumstances. But it worked out all right eventually, principally because, so far as I knew him—and that got to be pretty well—Cassidy was not amenable to circumstances. He beat them mostly, and some of them were pretty tough.

The circumstances surrounding our meeting were trying, because Cassidy was in bed after a hard day's work, and I aroused him at 3 a.m. by firing a revolver at his bulldog. His huts were on the railway works, and near the footpath to Jim Mackay's canteen—a pretty hot show. He used to be roused this way every Saturday and Sunday, and occasionally throughout the week, by visitors, black and white, warlike and friendly, thieving and sociable, but all drunk. At first he got a bulldog, but they got to know him, and after awhile the tip went round that half a pound

of beafsteak was a good buy and better than a
blunderbuss for Cassidy's Cutting. Then he
loaded fifty No. 12's with coarse salt, mixed with
pebbles and things, and, as he said to me afterwards :

' Ye were the fourth that night, and ye 'noyed
me wid yer swearin' an' shootin' an' that, so I just
passed the salt an' wint for the dust shot as bein'
more convincing like ; but the divil an' all of it
was, I couldn't get the cartridge in by reason of
drawin' the charge that was there already. Too
bad ! too bad ! for dust shot it was, av I'd only
known it, an' me thinkin' it was nothin' but salt.
Lord, Lord ! we're a miscontented lot ! Av it
wasn't for bein' greedy, I'd 've had ye wid the
dust shot safe as death. Faith, ye niver know
yer luck !'

That was all right from his point of view, but
as I had left my horse dying of Dikkop sickness
just this side of Kilo 26, and had walked along
the formation carrying saddle and bridle up to
Kilo 43—about ten miles—without a drink, and
twice lost my way between unconnected sections,
and twice walked over the ends of the formation
where culverts should have been and rolled down
twenty feet of embankment, and once got bogged
in a bottoming pit in a vlei, and many times
hacked my shins against wheelbarrows and piles

of picks stacked on the track, I think it was reasonable to let out at a bulldog that came at me like a hurricane out of the darkness and silence of 3 a.m. in the Bush veld, to say nothing of a half-finished railway cutting. And I think it only human to have cursed the owner with all my resources until the dog was called off.

I don't exactly know how it came about, but I slept in Cassidy's hut that night. He pushed me in before him, guiding me to the bed with a hand on each elbow. He said that there were no matches in the show and that it wasn't worth while looking for the candle, which, as he had no means of lighting it, I suppose it wasn't.

He had a rare brogue and a governing nasal drone, but it was the brogue that emboldened me to ask for whisky.

' Spirits !' said he ; ' not a drop, an' niver have; but jist sit ye where ye are, an' I'll fetch ye out some beer—Bass's, no less, av ye'll thry that ; and can dhrink from the bottle.'

He talked in jerks, and had a quaint knack of chucking remarks after an apparently completed sentence, evidently intending them to catch up to it and be tacked on. He dived under the bed somewhere, and a minute later I heard the squeaking of a corkscrew and the popping of a cork.

'Here y' are,' said he, as he pressed the bottle
into my two hands; 'drink hearty, me lad, and
praise yer God Dan O'Connell there's got too fat
an' lazy to pull ye down.'

I dare say he knew what he was talking about,
but, for my part, I confess that nothing in the
whole business had impressed me less than any
lack of earnestness on Dan O'Connell's part. I
sat awhile munching biscuits from a tin which he
had placed on the table and gurgling down beer
from the bottle. Cassidy was asleep. Ten
minutes passed, and I was finishing the beer,
when he sat up again, as I judged from the
sound, and remarked in a brisk, clear tone :

'Ye called me a mud-dollopin', dyke-diggin',
Amsterdam'd Dutchman ! Ye'll take back the
Dutchman, I believe ?'

'I will indeed,' I said, laughing.

'An' the mud ?'

'Yes, and the mud.'

He settled himself in the bunk again with a
grunt, and murmured in a tone of indignant
contempt :

'Mud, sez he, mud ! An' me shiftin' granite
boulders for soft rock, an shtruck solid formation
a fut from surface, an' getting two an' six a cubic
fer the lot ! Mud, faith ! An' not enough water
this three miles to the Crocodile to make spit for

an ant, barrin' what I can tap from the Figaro
Battery pipe! An' mud, sez he? Holy Fly!
Mud, be Gawd!'

It died away in a sleepy grunt, and Cassidy
was off. I groped about for a blanket, and, roll-
ing back into the meal-sack stretcher, forgot all
about mad Irishmen, sick horses, and earnest
bulldogs.

     *   *   *   *   *

One always experiences a curious sensation
on seeing by daylight that which one has only
known in the dark. Persons do for years a
certain journey or voyage, always starting and
always arriving at regular hours. One day
something happens which necessitates their passing in daylight the places formerly passed at
night. On such occasions even the most matter-
of-fact must marvel at the wanton freaks of their
imaginations. The real thing seems so inconceiv-
ably wrong after what the mind had pictured.
The appearance of a room, the outside of a house,
are ludicrously, hopelessly at variance with what
one had thought they should be. But it is, if
possible, worse when the subject is a person. I
have many times travelled with men at night by
coach, on horseback, on foot, and in a waggon;
have chatted sociably and exchanged all manner
of friendly turns; have slept at the same wayside

hotel, and in the morning found myself unable, until he spoke, to pick out of any two the one with whom I had spent hours the night before.

In the case of Cassidy the difference was appalling.

I awoke in such light as might leak through the grass hut; which was very little for light, but not bad for leakage.

The boy brought breakfast—coffee, bread, and cold venison, which suited me well—and I was turning my thoughts to the matter of a fresh horse for my homeward journey when I met the eye of one of my friends of the previous night. I say the eye, because I don't count the one in the black patch—I couldn't see it. But when Dan O'Connell stood in the doorway and allowed his one bloodshot, pink-rimmed eye to rest thoughtfully on me, it fairly fixed me. I used to recall his bandy legs and undershot jaw long afterwards whenever I thought of Cassidy's Cutting; but it was only when the luminous eye uprose before me that I used unconsciously to twitch about and draw my legs up as I did the morning I saw him in the flesh. Cassidy *was* a surprise; O'Connell wasn't. His appearance was only the cold chill of proof following a horrible conviction. I was much relieved when the boy cleared Dan out of the doorway with a bare-toed kick in the ribs and a vigorous 'Ow! Foosack!' I admired the boy for that, and even envied him.

Through the open doorway I saw a white man walking briskly towards the hut, and I stepped out to meet him. He was a man of medium height, but there was something in his walk and figure that arrested attention. I am sure I have never seen in any man such lithe, active movement and perfect symmetry. A close-fitting vest and a pair of white flannel trousers were what he wore. I remember that because, somehow, I always recall that first view in the morning light—the springy walk, the bare muscular arms, the curve of the chest, and the poise of the head, as the face was turned from me.

If I could tell this story without saying another word about his appearance, I would stop right here. I would greatly prefer to do so, but it is not possible. I hope no one will feel exactly as I felt when this man turned his face to me. It serves no good purpose to give revolting details, so I will only say that the man was disfigured—most horribly so.

I cannot recall what was said or done during the few minutes that passed after we met, but there are some impressions seared into my brain as with red-hot irons; there are some recollections which even now make me feel faint and dazed, and some which make me burn with shame. I take shame—bitter, burning shame—that I failed to grasp his outstretched hand, and that I let him read in my face the horror that seized me. It is one of those pitiful things that the longest lifetime is not long enough to let a man forget. Surging across this comes the vivid recollection of my conviction that this man was Cassidy. The first instant my glance lighted on him I felt what I can only call a sort of joyous conviction that it was he. I felt, in fact, that I recognised him. No doubt it seems odd, illogical, contradictory, even impossible, that, strong as the gratifying conviction was, the other, when he turned his face to me, was a thousand times stronger. It ought to have been a reversal of the first conviction. It wasn't. It was a smashing, terrible corroboration. It crushed me with a sense of personal affliction. It never germinated a doubt.

I had to stay all that day with him, and he was most gentle and courteous; most kindly and considerate. Every act heaped coals of fire on my ill-conditioned head. God knows I tried my best, but I could hardly look in his face, and I could not control my physical repugnance. I schooled myself to speak, and even to look, without betraying my thoughts, but I could not eat with him. I could not sit opposite a face half of which was gone; I could not use the plate, the cup, the fork, that he had used. I pleaded illness, and feigned it; but by night-time I was ill enough to need no feigning.

It was common enough for anyone benighted on those unhealthy flats to pay the penalty with a dose of fever. I got fever, and no one seemed surprised; but for the life of me I cannot even now help attaching some significance to the fact that I was certainly not ill before the scene at the hut door.

I lay in that grass hut for a week or more, some of the time delirious—all the time panting with fever and shivering with ague; tossing wakefully and gasping for air; complaining of everything, unutterably miserable and despondent; hating the sight of food, shrinking from each act of kindness, scowling at the sound of a voice. My case was not worse than hundreds of others. I mention these things only to make clear what I mean when I say that never at any moment during that time did I awake or want anything but Cassidy was there to tend me. His was the care, the watchfulness, the gentleness, of a good woman. Can one say more?

It is odd that during that time I only saw him as he ought to have been—as I am sure at one

time he had been—a man whose countenance
matched his character. It is not so odd, perhaps,
that as I recovered and became rational the
feeling of repulsion did not return, only an infinite
pity for a hardly-stricken fellow-creature whose
physical endowments and whose prospects must
have been far above the average, and whose affliction was proportionately great.

When I left there was one feeling that was
stronger than simple gratitude to him. It was
thankfulness that something had occurred to
prevent me from leaving with only horror and
repulsion. I was thankful for the sickness that
left me richer by a heart full of pity and—I think
the right word is—reverence !

*   *   *   *   *

My lines were laid in other places than
Cassidy's, and as months passed by without my
either seeing or hearing of him, I might, for
aught I know, have forgotten him, or come to
recall him only as one recalls, after lapse of
years, some curious experience. This *might* have
happened, I say; but it didn't. Mainly because
of a conversation which revived my keenest interest in him.

Several of us had walked out to dine and spend
the evening at the Chaunceys', and as we sat on
the stoep smoking and chatting, the ladies being

with us, the conversation turned on a concert or entertainment of some kind which was being got up for the relief of some distressed families in the place. Somebody hazarded the opinion that the 'distressed family' business was being somewhat overdone, and that there was no evidence of it as far as he had been able to see.

The remark was unfortunate, for Mrs. Chauncey happened to be one of the promoters of the charity. She—good little woman !—had her young matron's soul full of sympathy still ; her store had not been plundered by impostors, and she vehemently defended her project. She did more ; she carried war and rout into the enemy's quarters and surmised that men, young men, whose lives are divided between money-making and pleasure-seeking, are not the best judges of what those who keep their troubles to themselves may have to endure.

'When you' (the young men) 'are settling differences on shares or cards, or having your occasional splits—or whatever else you do all day long—there are women and children aching for one good meal, shrinking back for want of ordinary clothing, languishing and dropping for want of a man's arm to fend and support them.'

Jack Chauncey — good chap ! — must have thought this from his wife just a wee bit spirited, for, after a pause, he gently drew a herring across the trail.

'By - the - by, dear,' he asked thoughtfully, 'what became of that good-looking young widow who came here with her kid and looked so jolly miserable ? By Gad ! her face has been haunting me ever since. Did you manage anything for her ?'

'You mean Mrs. Mallandane. She would not take anything. She wanted to work; to earn, not to beg, she said. I have managed to get her some needlework, but, oh, so little, poor thing ! And the pay is too dreadful ! Now, there is a case in point. A widow, absolutely penniless, with a child of four or five to support. A woman of education and breeding, without a friend in the world, apparently; shunned by everyone—by some on account of her poverty, by others for her good looks and reserve. She certainly is difficult to approach. I have been to her now four times, and it was only on the last occasion that she thawed enough to tell me anything of herself. She has lived for years on what she believed to be the proceeds of her husband's estate. Until within the last few months she was under this impression. But something happened which made her suspicious, and she found out that the income left by her husband was pure fiction, and that what she had been living on was an allowance from the only real friend she or her husband ever had— the man who was her husband's partner when he died.'

' Does she say that her husband is dead?' asked Carter, the unfortunate ' young man ' who had before provoked Mrs. Chauncey's ire.

Carter was very young, and I could see that he had no *arrière pensée* in asking that question. He did not mean to be impertinent. But I could also see that Mrs. Chauncey did not take that view. Her little iced reply finished poor Carter.

' I said that she was a widow, Mr. Carter, and I do not care to make another's misfortunes the subject of an argument.'

I felt sorry for Carter, he was such an ass ; and I believe the other two fellows pitied him also ; so we did not refer to the subject as we walked home together in the moonlight. That, however, did not suit Carter. After awhile he gave an uncomfortable laugh, and said :

' The little woman was rather down on me to-night about the charity show. I rather put my foot in it, I think.'

' Think !' said Lawton (one of our party), with heavy contempt. ' Think ! I wonder you claim to be able to think ! I never in my life saw any- one make such a blighted idiot of himself !'

'Dash it all, man! give me a chance. The
"distressed family" allusion was unlucky, I admit;
but I hadn't the faintest intention of returning to
the subject when I asked about the husband.
Man alive! Why, the nerve of the Mallandane
woman fairly knocked the breath out of me. The
cheek of her cramming poor Mrs. Chauncey with
yarns of her husband's death and estate, when
everyone knows that he isn't dead at all; that
she gave him the slip, and went off with the
"only friend"—his partner! A man with half
his face eaten away by disease. I've seen the
fellow at the house myself. Old Larkin, of the
Bank, knew them in Kimberley. They were
claim-holders and contractors there and used to
bank with him. The firm was Cassidy and
Mallandane. I only wonder she continues to call
herself Mallandane. It's a formality she might
as well have dispensed with.'

I knew Carter to be a gossipy young devil, so
I held my peace about Cassidy; but it was with
an effort. My impulse was to give Carter the
lie direct, but I remembered Mrs. Chauncey's last
words and refrained.

We walked along in silence, and after a while
Carter stopped in the road opposite a small
house, the door of which stood partly open.
There were voices outside, and as Carter said,

'Hush! listen!' we stopped instinctively, and my heart sank as I recognised a voice that said 'Good-night.' I moved on hastily, disgusted at being trapped into eavesdropping, and Carter laughed.

'That's the only friend! There's no mistaking *that*. But I wonder why he's coming away,' said the youth, with unmistakable and insinuating emphasis on the last words.

No one answered his self-satisfied cackling. I was listening to the brisk walk behind us. I would have known it in a million. Closer and closer it came; his sleeve brushed mine as he stepped lightly past. I let him go, and I don't know why. But I felt like a whipped cur for doing it.

It seemed to me that I must heretofore have been living in extraordinary ignorance of what was going on round about me in a small place; for, as though it only needed the start, from the first mention of this story by Carter I was always hearing it, or a similar one, or one half corroborating it.

I made an effort to see Cassidy the first thing next morning, but he had left his hotel—presumably having gone out to the works again. After a day or two had passed I felt glad that I had not met him—glad because I felt sure that he would have noticed that there was something wrong. He would instinctively have detected the cordiality and confidence which were controlled by an effort of will, and were not—as they should have been, and as they did again become—spontaneous and real.

This worried me exceedingly and I turned it over and over again to get at the truth, and eventually it came to this. I knew that they were right as to the cause of his disfigurement; it was impossible to look at him and not accept it. I had no high moral prejudices about this. I only pitied him the more. But I did not believe a word of the rest of the story. All presumption and a heap of circumstances were against me, but I am glad to say that, but for the first hesitation, I never, never doubted him.

It may have been a week or two after this that I met Mrs. Chauncey in camp one afternoon. I had not seen her since the evening already referred to, and, as it was an off afternoon, I asked leave to join her in her walk home.

We wandered on slowly through the outskirts of the camp, along the most direct road to the Chaunceys' house. Since I had heard and seen what I had that evening my interest in Mrs. Mallandane had increased. I never passed the house without looking. I claim—even to myself—that it was real interest and not curiosity that prompted me. Once or twice I had seen the figure in simple black, but not sufficiently clearly to have known the face again. Her figure I don't think I should have mistaken ; it was rather striking. There was also a little girl who used to sit under a mimosa-tree studying her lessons or doing sums on a slate. She and I became friends. I was drawn to the youngster because, when passing one day, I took the unwarrantable liberty of looking over her shoulder to see what the sum was. After a decent pause, during which I might have taken the hint, she turned up at me a very serious little face lighted by large blue eyes, and lisped slowly :

'I don't like people to thtand behind, becauth I fordet my thums.'

I laughingly patted the little head, and went on ; but after this I always stopped to chaff my little friend about her ' thums,' and I generally brought an offering of some sort—sweets, cake, or fruit.

Thinking of the house and its people as we walked along, I was not sorry when Mrs. Chauncey asked if I would mind waiting for a minute or two while she went in to see her *protégée* about some work secured or promised.

I sat down in my little friend's seat and waited. I had not long to wait. Presently I heard behind

me the awkward tiptoeing of a child trying to
walk very silently.   Like Brer Rabbit, I lay low.
Then came the climbing on to the seat, and finally
a pair of childish hands were clapped over my
eyes to an accompaniment of half-suppressed
squeals of laughter, broken by panting efforts to
maintain the blind-folding hug.   I was busily
keeping up the illusion by extravagantly bad
guesses as to who it was, when I heard the
rustle of a dress, and someone ran out, calling :

'Molly, Molly ! how can you be so naughty,
darling ?   Oh, do excuse her !'

I was released.   My hat was in the dust and
my hair rumpled.   I saw Mrs. Chauncey in the
background in peals of laughter ; Mrs. Mallandane
before me, looking most concerned, and holding
the bewildered Molly by the hand ; and Molly
vindicating herself by saying with much dignity :

'Mother, it's only the gentimell that dooth
my thumth an' kitheth me.'

As a defence this was, of course, adequate—not
to say excellent ; but it was rather embarrassing
for me.   It was so effective, however, that I was
spared the necessity of saying anything myself.
Mrs. Chauncey introduced me to her *protégée* as
she would have done to any of her lady friends,
and the *protégée* bowed, as it seemed to me, with
a great deal more grace and quite as much easy

composure as the best of them. That was my
first thought. The next was to take myself in-
dignantly to task for instituting a comparison.

As we resumed our walk I was wondering what
could be the tie between this woman and Cassidy.
There was no mistaking her class. She was a
gentlewoman to her finger-tips. I was roused
from my rather discourteous distraction by Mrs.
Chauncey saying :

'You are not so surprised now, perhaps, that
I lost my temper with Mr. Carter the other
evening. I am sorry I spoke as I did, but I felt
it deeply—indeed I did.'

'I can well understand it,' I answered.

'How do you like her ?' she asked abruptly.

'What ! after an interview of two minutes—
and such an interview ?'

Mrs. Chauncey smiled, and said :

'Well, I only wanted to know your impression.
And, after all, you have had time to form one, for
you have been thinking of her all the time since
we left the house !'

'Perfectly true—I have. And to speak candidly, I think I have seldom—indeed, I think,
never—seen a face that interested me more ;
partly, I suppose, because of what you told us.
And I don't think I have ever seen anyone look so
infinitely sad. It is a pitiful, haunting face.'

'I feel that also. I have never been able to forget her look since she came to me a month ago for work—needlework or any work. I will never believe that she could be an impostor. No, no ! Truth is stamped in her face — truth and sorrow.'

I had always liked Mrs. Chauncey. Just at that moment I was mentally patting her on the back and calling her 'a little brick,' for it was clear that she too had heard something—heard it and passed it by. Good woman !

I was a bachelor, and not too old to feel ; and, over and above my interest in Cassidy, this whole affair fascinated me considerably. From this time forward I never passed the house without greeting mother or child with sincere warmth, or missing them with an equally genuine sense of disappointment. I never met Mrs. Chauncey without inquiring with interest the latest news of her friend and all details of her affairs.

There was never much to tell. Now it was some commission for a dress, now the mending of children's clothes—another time the trimming of hats or working a tennis-net, that helped to make ends meet without hurt to her pride. These were petty details which might pass in woman's chat, but should fail to interest a man, you would think. Nevertheless, they interested me. They did more. In the evenings, as I sat alone and smoked out in the starlight they helped me to conjure up pictures and to see her as she would at those very moments, perhaps, be employed.

I would have done anything to help her had I been able, but there was nothing I could do. I had even learned that I might not as much as evince sympathy or interest, except at the cost of insult to her. On one occasion when I happened to meet and walk with her in one of the main streets of the camp, I was frigidly cut by two ladies with whom I thought I was on quite friendly terms. This disturbed me considerably, not on my own account, but because of the insult and injustice to one who was powerless to resent it. It hurt me even more to realize that it would be wise to bow before this and prove greater friendship by showing less.

I was still smarting under this next morning when I was accosted by one of those puddle-headed, blundering idiots of whom there seem to be one or more in any community, no matter how small.

'I say, old chap,' he began, 'look here, ye know! You're not playin' the game, ye know, old chap! The missis has been complainin' to me about you. You know what I mean.'

I detest this 'dontcherknow,' 'g'-dropping

kind of animal at any time — the thing that
fondles you with ' old chap ' and ' dear boy ' and
refers to its wife as ' the missis.'   But apart from
this, I was to-day especially unprepared to submit
to further outrage.   I was still smarting, as I said
before.

'My good man,' I said, ' may I ask you to be
more explicit ?'

'Why, dash it all, old chap ! you know what I
mean—er.   It's no affair of mine, of course, if you
only keep it quiet, don't you know.   But you
don't give one a chance, don't you know ; and,
after all, you can't run with the hare and hunt
with the hounds, and all that sort of thing, don't
you know !'

I was trying to keep my temper, but with no
very marked success, I fear ; but I said as calmly
as I could :

'That's a very original remark, my friend, and
no doubt equally intelligent, but I shall be pleased
if you will be good enough to apply it so that *I*
can understand it.'

'Look here, old chap.   If you will go and walk
in broad daylight with a woman like that, you
know—well, you can't expect——'

'Stop now !'   I said.   I had hardly breath
enough to speak, and there must have been something unpleasant in my face, for he stepped back

a pace or two. 'So far you are only a babbling
fool. If you go on now you will be an infernal
cad and must take the consequences. You
understand what I mean. And further, as you
have been good enough to hint that I should
choose my line, I may tell you—to adopt your
happy illustration—that I elect to "run with the
hare." You see! Perhaps *you* understand what
I mean!'

Now, before two minutes had passed, I did not
need anyone to tell me that I had done the worst
and most unwise thing possible under the circumstances. Of course I knew well enough that
when a woman is concerned two things are very
essential—that the man shall keep his temper,
and that he shall be judicious, even circumspect,
in defending. Having failed in the former, I
necessarily failed in the latter, and I felt sick
with impotent rage when I realized it.

I knew how the story would circulate, and I
knew exactly how it would be touched up,
amplified, and illustrated with graphic gesticula-
tions when it reached the club and Exchange and
passed through the hands of certain expert *racon-
teurs*; and to avoid the lamentable result of chaff
and further provocation I got away for a couple of
days to give myself—and the story—a chance.

Several weeks passed after this incident, during

which I saw but little of Mrs. Mallandane, and
heard not much more. Occasionally I heard of
Cassidy from men coming up the line. In spite
of his grumbling and seeming discontent with the
nature of the country in his section nobody
believed that Cassidy's Cutting was such a very
unprofitable job as he gave out. Cassidy was too
old a hand to be drawn into any admission
which could be used against him for the purpose
of cutting down prices in future contracts. Those
best able to judge put him down to make close on
£10,000 out of that job. His section lay some
sixty miles from Barberton, and, as far as I
knew, he had been into camp only twice during
the five months that had passed since I had first
met him. One occasion was the night on which
I had seen him; the other when he called at the
office to see me. I was out of camp that day
and missed him. I do not know how often he
may have been in besides those two occasions.

Mrs. Chauncey and I were real friends. Jack
was one of my oldest chums, and when he
married I found—what does not necessarily
follow—that his wife was just one to strengthen
the friendship and not weaken it. With regard
to her, I felt that if an occasion should arise requiring that I should make a confidante of any
woman Mrs. Chauncey would be the one. I

don't know that I ever realized this sufficiently
forcibly to express it even to myself until after
a remark which she made to me about this time.

She had been telling me some little thing about
Mrs. Mallandane, and I may have shown by my
attention — perhaps even by questions — more
interest than she expected or thought called for.
There was quite a long silence, during which
I felt that she was thinking of something con-
cerning me. When she turned towards me her
expression was one of almost tender consideration,
and in the gentlest possible voice she said :

'It is good to be kind and generous, and to
help those who need it ; but when a man means
to help a woman it should be clear to him from
day to day, from hour to hour, not only how far *he*
means to go, but also what she will understand.'

The words went home to me, and I suppose I
showed it, for she added a little nervously :

'You must not mind that from me. " Faithful
are the wounds of a friend." '

'Taken as meant, Mrs. Chauncey ; and—thank
you !' I meant it.

I made a careful and impartial examination of
conscience that night when I had the silence and
darkness to favour me ; and although I honestly
acquitted myself, there was just the faintest suggestion of the finding of the Irish jury : 'We find

the prisoner not guilty; but he's not to do it again.'
I told myself again that Mrs. Chauncey was a
'little brick' for her timely and well-judged
warning; for I thought it was quite possible that
I might have drifted on and 'gone soft' before
knowing it. I am satisfied that there was no
cause for alarm, as the resolution to 'ease up'
cost me neither effort nor pang.

I abided fairly by the spirit of my unspoken
pact. I changed my daily route to one that did
not lead past Mrs. Mallandane's house. I ceased
to talk of her; I even tried not to think of her.
But just there I failed—for the effort to forget
makes occasion to remember.

*　　*　　*　　*　　*

It was the tail end of summer. The heat was
terrible, and in all the outlying parts—even in
the lower portions of the camp—malarial fever was
prevalent. The accounts from the line were par-
ticularly bad, nearly all the engineers, contractors, and sub-contractors being more or less
laid up by attacks of the summer fiend. One of
the engineers suffering from a mild attack was
brought in, and, being at the hotel when he
arrived, I heard accounts of what was going on.
He told me that Cassidy had had attack after
attack, but that he would neither lie up there nor
come into hospital. It was work, work, work,

with him, all day and night, except when he was looking after others—and, in truth, his camp was a kind of improvised hospital. Cassidy, he said, with his superb strength and physique would not give in. He would not believe that fever could beat a man who was game, and he fought it.

There was no suitable conveyance to be got before night, so I arranged to start after dark, for I was determined to do something to repay the kindness I had had at Cassidy's hands. I took a serious view of his case, for I knew how these things usually ended, and he was not going to die without an effort on my part to save him.

I walked home that night worrying considerably about poor Cassidy and wishing to Heaven that the trap was ready to start at once. I had reached the crossing-stones in the little stream, where my old and new paths forked out. It was dusk, and I was not thinking of whom I might meet, so I started at the sight of Mrs. Mallandane a few paces off coming towards me, evidently to meet me.

'Oh, I have waited for hours to meet you!' she began without any ceremony, and talking nervously and fast. 'I thought you had gone already, and yet I feared to annoy you by going to your office. Look here—look! Tell me, is this true? Oh, you can't see—I forgot; it's too dark. Here in

the paper they say you are going down the line
to-night to bring in someone who is ill, very ill
with fever. Tell me, is it true ?'

' It is quite true. I leave to-night after nine,'
I answered—I hope without betraying surprise ;
but I could not help noticing that she did not
mention Cassidy's name, and that she was painfully excited. I drew no conclusions—I had no
time for thought; but these things left a weight
on my heart for all that, and it was not lightened
as she went on.

' I have come to ask you something. You will
please bring him to my house. I must nurse him!
He must come to me !' This was not a favour
sought, it was rather a direction given, and there
was only the slightest note of interrogation in her
voice. I could only repeat in surprise :

' To your house, Mrs. Mallandane ?'

' Yes—yes ! You will do that for me, please ?'

' I am sorry, but I do not think that would be
right. His place is clearly in the hospital, and I
have no right to take him elsewhere.'

' You refuse ? Oh, you cannot refuse me !'

' Mrs. Mallandane, you put it very harshly.
You must see that I cannot do otherwise. I
know of nothing to justify me in not sending him
to hospital. It will be better for him, and far
better for you.'

She drew a sharp breath and faced me drawn up to her full height, looking me straight in the eyes.

'I half expected this,' she said. 'I only asked you because I feared to worry him. Your refusal is nothing. He will come to me all the same. You will not refuse to take a letter to him, will you, if I detain you a few minutes longer?'

We were quite close to her little cottage, and as we walked towards it I tried to soften my refusal as best I could. She, however, did not seem to hear me.

She left me seated in the little parlour. There was no light in the room, but she carried in a lamp from an adjoining one; and I have never been so struck by a face as I was by hers when the glow of the lamp lighted it up. The charm of her beauty was not one whit abated—for beautiful she was; and yet there was only one thing to be read in her face, and that was resolution. It lay in her lips, the curve of the nostrils, a peculiar look in the eye, and a certain poise of the head. In very truth, she looked superb.

I sat waiting while the minutes passed, and not a sound broke the perfect silence in the house. Everything was so still that it seemed as if there could be no one within miles of me.

There was a book on the table before me, and I
took it up unthinkingly.   It opened where a
cabinet-sized photograph had been left in it—as a
marker I suppose.   The photograph showed the
head and shoulders of a man, and the face shown
in full was one of the gayest and most resolute
that I ever remember to have seen.   There was
something very attractive about it, and there was,
as I thought, a faint suggestion of somebody I
had known or seen.   It was a *good* face, splendidly
strong and honest, and, from a man's point of
view, a right handsome face too.

To look at a photograph uninvited may be an
impertinence ; to read the inscription on the back
certainly is.   And yet these are things which one
is apt to do unthinkingly and even instinctively.
I turned the photograph round and read :

' O death, where is thy sting ?   O grave, where
is thy victory ?' and under that a date.   I put it
back in the book, feeling that I had been prying
into the secrets of a woman's grief.

Presently I heard a chair pushed back in the
next room and Mrs. Mallandane's step approaching.
She handed me a closed note.

' You will give that to him, please,' she said
politely, but very firmly.   ' He will come here if
he receives it ; but it is possible that he may
still be delirious, and if so, I only ask you again

if you will be good enough to bring him to me.'

With the knowledge which after-events have given me it is difficult to say whether I was concerned only for Cassidy's health and Mrs. Mallandane's good name, or whether I was not pricked to anxiety by some other feeling. My heart did sink at her suggestion, I don't know whether through selfishness or something better. I felt that I was beginning to yield before her evident purpose, but my answer was evasive. I said I did not see how I could promise anything.

She waved that impatiently aside. I recall the motion of her hand, as though she could literally brush such things away. She came a step nearer to me, the light shone full in her face, on the waves of her hair, on her slightly-parted lips, and glinted and flashed back from her eyes. For half a minute she stood so looking at me, and I was conscious of the grip of her hand on the back of a chair, and of the rise and fall of her breast as she breathed.

'You know him! You have seen him?' she queried in a low, deliberate voice.

'Yes,' I answered.

'You know he is disfigured?'

I could barely answer again, ' Yes.'

'When I tell you, then, that *I am the cause of*

that, will you deny me the privilege of any
reparation I can make ?'

The words met me like a blow in the face. I
was crushed ! God knows what I would have
done but that I saw the flame of colour that
leapt into her face, and the trembling and quivering of her lips. I gasped out :

' No, no ! I will do it.'

She seemed so upset, so unsteady, that I made
a half-step towards her, but she motioned me
back, saying :

' Go now—go ! Please go, and leave me.'

A hundred thoughts were surging and churning
in my head as I drove down the long, long valley
of the Lampogwana River that night. I felt as
miserable as man need feel. Everything seemed
wrong—most of it horribly so—but turn as I
might from one phase to another, the one thing
always recurred, pervading, dominating everything : ' I am the cause of that.' The words
rang in my ears again and again, and the horrible
significance shamed me afresh each time, always
to be answered by something which said, ' No,
I will believe ! I will trust !'

Poor Cassidy was very, very bad when I reached
him, and his lucid intervals were far between.
His appearance was terrible, the ghastly pallor
adding, as I had thought nothing could add, to

the face from which one eye, the nose, half the
upper lip, and portion of one cheek, were gone.
It was terrible—truly terrible !

There is no need to dwell on it all. I got him
in and he lived for five days. Fever didn't kill
him ; it couldn't have ; he was too strong and too
stout-hearted. It was hæmorrhage resulting from
some old injury received in an accident years before.
The doctor told me that when the artery had gone
Cassidy knew he would be dead in a few minutes.
He begged the doctor to leave him, and turning
to Mrs. Mallandane, asked her to cover his face
with a handkerchief, and to hold his hand. He
said to her, ' God bless you, Molly ! Good-bye !'
and died like the man he was.

Mrs. Chauncey was the real friend in that time
of need. It was she who had supplied everything
that an invalid could want ; it was she who stayed
all that long night through with Mrs. Mallandane,
who went with her to the funeral and stood by
her, and stayed with her when all was over.

The day after the funeral I sat in my office
dazed and stupefied with worrying and puzzling
over many things in connection with these people
whose affairs and whose lives seemed to have
become suddenly entangled with mine. Not the
least of my worries was the document before me,
which was Cassidy's will : ' I give everything

absolutely to Mary Mallandane,' and nominating
me as his executor.

I dreaded the first interview—so much so, in
fact, that I got Mrs. Chauncey to go with me.
The tall black figure and the excessive pallor of
her face smote very hard on my heart, but I was
relieved by the presence of little Molly, who stuck
to me from the time I entered the room until
Mrs. Mallandane sent her away. I had already
stated my object in calling when she sent Molly
out, and I was about to resume, when she asked
me abruptly :

' Do you know anything of his past life ?'

' Nothing whatever,' I said.

' Nor of mine ?'

' No, Mrs. Mallandane.'

She laid a hand on one of Mrs. Chauncey's, who
was sitting near, and said gravely :

' You, who have been my friend, know nothing
either. It is right that you should—that you
both should.'

We were sitting at a table in the parlour ; the
writing materials were lying on it ready for my
use. The two ladies sat close together opposite me.

I cannot give Mrs. Mallandane's own words,
nor can I convey her manner when telling us the
story of her life. Sometimes she would talk in a
subdued monotone, telling, with an absence of

feeling that was infinitely pathetic, of their troubles. Sometimes she would be roused to a pitch of feeling that left her voice but a husky whisper. Once—just once—I fancied there was the faintest trace of contempt in her tone when referring to—well, not to Cassidy. If it was so, it was at any rate instantly lost in a flow of pity.

This is substantially what she told us. Mallandane and Cassidy had owned claims in the Kimberley or one of the neighbouring mines, and were in fact partners doing business together. They were both young Irishmen, and had come out on the same boat some years before—which were considered sufficient reasons for their entering into partnership. Cassidy was the one with the brains, money, and work; and, from what I gathered, there seems to have been no reason, except Cassidy's good-nature, for the alliance with Mallandane at all. However, they prospered, and Mallandane went home for a trip, and married and brought his wife back to Kimberley.

For a couple of years all went well—in fact, until the firm began to lose money. Reverses only stimulated Cassidy to harder work and more cheery, indomitable effort. You couldn't beat him. But it was different with Mallandane. All his wife said was that he lost heart; used to go away day after day and night after night to

11

where he could forget his worries—drinking and
gambling. When Cassidy first recognised that
his partner was falling, he gave up his own house,
suggesting that it would be doing him (Cassidy)
a good turn if they would let him board with
them. He gave himself up to a splendid effort to
save his partner from ruin.

For a time it answered, but Mallandane, besides
being naturally unstable, must have been bitten
by drink, for he broke out again, and nothing
either wife or friend could do could save him.
There came scenes—brutality and insult to the
wife, ingratitude and insult to the friend. She
told us nothing except in pity and forgiveness of
her dead husband—nothing, that is, that justice
to Cassidy did not require; but it is not difficult
to imagine what happened, and, indeed, I know
now that it was only the pitiful helplessness of
the wife and child, and the knowledge that his
presence was food, and even life, to them, that
held Cassidy to his partner; for in his fits of
drunkenness Mallandane would have murdered
both wife and child.

Cassidy worked from four in the morning until
eight at night, and at times through the day he
would run up from the claims to the house, to see
that all was well. All he made went to keep the
house going, and it was given as a matter of

course. No complaint was made, although Mallandane now ceased even the pretence of work and spent the whole day in the canteens.

But the end came when least expected. Mallandane, when he did come home at all, did not get up until hours after Cassidy was at work. He used to awake drunk and dazed, and wander off at once, unshaven, dirty and half dressed, to the nearest canteen.

One morning, however, there was a change. He was gray-faced, puffy and sodden, it is true, but he fussed about the house briskly, talking to himself. He got out a clean moleskin suit, and told the servant that he could not wait for breakfast, as he had to fire the eight o'clock shots, and the holes were all charged and waiting for him.

Within a quarter of an hour Cassidy had come up for breakfast. Mrs. Mallandane met him on the way and told him what the servant had in the meantime told her; and Cassidy raced back to stop his delirious partner. With a madman's cunning and instinct he had slipped down the mine from ledge to ledge and along dangerous slopes until he reached the lowest workings, and when Cassidy, after some delay in getting a bucket on the hauling-gear to go down in, reached the spot, the boys told him that Mallandane 'umtagati' (bewitched) had gone into the

drive to fire the charges, and would let no one go
near him.

Cassidy looked at the black mouth of the drive.
He did not think of the worthless sodden wretch
who had gone in there. He recalled the partner
of years, the mate of good times and bad, and he
recalled, too, the horror-stricken look on the face
of the woman he had just left. He dashed in to
the sound of a warning yell from every man in
the mine.

When occasion calls there is still no lack of
brave men. Heroes spring into recognition from
every grade of life, from every class of material;
and while the half-dozen explosions still echoed
and reverberated in the circle of the mine, there
were men dashing in to the rescue at the
imminent risk of their lives, heedless of the
deadly fumes and of possible unexploded charges.

'The firm' lay in one heap—Cassidy on his
back, Mallandane athwart him. To the only
person to whom he ever spoke of the affair,
Cassidy said: 'He was stooping to light another
fuse when I reached him. I gripped both arms
round him as he turned on me and tried to
carry him out. It was a wrestling match, for he
showed fight. My face was over his one shoulder,
as his was over mine; but mine was turned
towards the shots.'

A piece of the rock that shattered poor Cassidy's face entered the back of his partner's head, and *he* never stirred again.

Cassidy lay for months in hospital, bandaged, blindfolded, barely alive; and the woman he had stood by, stood by him. When he was able to walk about, it was on her arm he leaned. When he was fit to leave, it was to her house he went to be tended for months longer. He never complained nor lost heart, although he knew that one eye was gone and thought he would lose the other.

Some seven or eight months had passed, and he was getting well and strong—he was healing. She had always dreaded the effect of the first sight of himself, and for this reason had removed the mirrors from the rooms he frequented; but one day, when she had been out for a while, she found him lying on the sofa, the bandage off his eyes, and a hand-glass dropped on the carpet close by. It was the only time he had fainted or in any way given in.

Later in the evening he said :

'I don't really mind so much now that I know. It was the suspense that worried me.' And, after a pause, he added in a voice that seemed to let you *hear* his heart lifting : 'I'll be able to tackle work again soon, and will be all right again.'

'That was the only allusion,' Mrs. Mallandane said, 'that he ever made to his disfigurement. I believe it was out of delicacy and consideration for my feelings that he never spoke about it. You could not even see that he ever thought of it, for he had that splendid manliness that doesn't know what self-consciousness means.

'Only one thing showed unmistakably that he did feel it, and that he felt he was dead to all the promise of his past. You must have remarked his manner of speech ?' she observed, turning to me. 'He spoke like a working man. *That* was his only shield. He deliberately sank himself to that level to be spared the prominence and pity that would be given him as a gentleman. It was his hope to pass through life unnoticed. With me, and with me only, he had no disguise, no concealment, no reserve !'

He used always to talk of their affairs as one and the same, in order to keep up the illusion he had encouraged in her from the beginning when he had told her very seriously that 'it would never do to liquidate the firm's business now. It would mean sacrificing *everything*.' She agreed to do whatever he thought right ; and at the end of every month he used to hand to her, scrupulously accounted for, a sum greater or less, according to ' the firm's profits for the month.'

From his own 'profits' he always managed to have something—no matter how little—to spend on Molly, who was his pet and companion always. The proceeds of the sale of house and furniture— when they had to be given up—were handed over to Mrs. Mallandane 'for a stand-by,' and she went into lodgings because she 'would feel more comfortable and have more time to give to Molly there'—not because he was watchful over her good name and would not stay in the house once he was well enough to walk alone.

When Cassidy extended the firm's 'business'— that is to say, went to the Cape Colony, Natal, and Transvaal, in search of contracts on the various railway lines—he continued to remit the 'profits' with the most elaborate statements, which Mrs. Mallandane, as a partner, felt bound to study, and, as a woman, often wept over in despair.

This had gone on for several years, and it was not until after she had gone to Barberton, 'to be near the business,' that something had made her suspicious that the joint capital locked up in the business was all a generous imposition.

'It only needed the suggestion,' said Mrs. Mallandane, 'to show me an appalling chain of evidence—evidence of his generosity and patient tactful help—evidence of my blind content and foolishness. I spoke to him when next he came in. He could see that I knew, and he simply said that " Ralph would have done the same for him." God forgive me! He gave up his life to me! He suffered living death for me! He lived when it would have been a million mercies to have died. He bore all that man could bear and never grudged it. And I—I cut his heart in two when I refused his help! I know it! I wished I had died before I got the look he gave me when I told him that I could not take his help. Month after month went by and he did not come to me —he, who used to be here on the first day of every month. But I knew he was near. Twice I saw him passing slowly by at night when he had come to watch over us. The first time I was too surprised to call. The second time I called him and he came to me. He stayed until late that evening ; and he went away happy again because we registered our second compact : that if we (Molly and I) were ever in real need I would send for him ; that if he were sick or in need of friends the privilege of friends should be ours.'

She stopped for quite a while, and when she spoke again her voice trembled and it was all she could do to control it so that she could speak at all. I could not bear to look in her face.

'You two have seen him,' she said, and, turning to me, added, 'You have known him. I have liked to tell you all about him; and I like to tell you now that I know he loved me—that I think it is the greatest honour a woman can have to be loved by such a man: for not any woman that I have ever known, or heard of, or read of, was good enough for him!'

She left the room for a moment, and returning laid something on the table before us, saying :

'You remember him as you saw him. Try— try to think of him as I do—like *this!* It is all you can do for the memory of a good and honourable man.'

It was the photograph I had seen in her book the day I left to bring him in.

*   *   *   *   *

All those things happened some years ago.

Out on the grass there, in front of my window, there is a little girl trying to dissuade a very small boy from· pulling the black ear off an old white bulldog; but the fat little fists keep their grip, and as he staggers under the effort the little chap says :

'Molly mus' pull Dan'l Conn'l olla ear! *Make* him det up !'

Watching them with the brightest, merriest smile in the world, and looking years younger than when I first saw her, Mrs.——

But if I mentioned her name this would not be an anonymous story.

THE POOL.

EVERYONE remembers the rush to De Kaap some years ago. How everyone said that everyone else would make fortunes in half no time, and the country would be saved! Well, my brother Jim and I thought we would like to make fortunes too; so we packed our boxes, donned flannel shirts, felt hats and moleskin trousers, with a revolver each carelessly slung at our sides, and started. We intended to dig for about a year or so, and then sell out and live on the interest of our money—£30,000 each would do. It was all cut and dried. I often almost wished it wasn't so certain, as now one hadn't a chance of coming back suddenly and *surprising* the loved ones at home with the news of a grand fortune.

Full of excitement (certainties notwithstanding) we went down to Kent's Forwarding Store, and there met Mr. Harding, whose waggons were loaded for the gold-fields. This was our chance, and we took it.

On November 10, 1883, we crossed Little Sunday's River and outspanned at the foot of Knight's Cutting. The day was close and sultry, and Harding thought it best to lie by until the cool of the evening before attempting the hill. It wasn't much of a cool evening we got after all ; except that we had not the scorching rays of the sun beating down upon us, it was no cooler at 10 p.m. than at mid-day. We were outspanned above the cutting, and the oppressive heat of the day and the sultriness of the evening seemed to have told on our party, and we were all squatted about on the long soft grass, smoking or thinking. Besides my brother and myself there were two young Scotchmen (just out from home) and a little Frenchman. He was a general favourite on account of his inexhaustible good-nature and un- flagging high spirits.

We were, as I have said, stretched out on the grass smoking in silence, watching the puffs and rings of smoke melt quietly away, so still was the air. How long we had lain thus I don't know, but I was the first to break the silence by exclaiming :

' What a grand night for a bathe !'

There was no reply to this for some seconds. and then Jim gave an apathetic grunt in courteous recognition of the fact that I had spoken. I subsided again, and there was another long silence—evidently no one wanted to talk ; but I had become restless and fidgety under the heat and stillness, and presently I returned to the charge.

' Who's for a bathe ?' I asked.

Someone grunted out something about ' no place.'

' Oh yes, there is,' said I, glad of even so much encouragement ; and then, turning to Harding, I said :

' I hear the water in the kloof. There is a place, isn't there ?'

' Yes,' he answered slowly, ' there is *one* place, but you wouldn't care to dip there. . . . It's the Murderer's Pool.'

' The what ?' we asked in a breath.

' The Murderer's Pool,' he repeated with such slow seriousness that we at once became interested —the name sent an odd tingle through one. I was already all attention, and during the pause that followed the others closed around and settled themselves to hear the yarn. When he had tantalized us enough with his provoking slowness, Harding began :

' About this time last year—— By-the-by, what is the date ?' he asked, breaking off.

' The tenth !' exclaimed two or three together.

'By Jove! it's the very day. Yes, that's
queer. This very day last year I was outspanned
on this spot, as we are now. I had a lady and
gentleman with me as passengers that trip. They
were pleasant, accommodating people, and gave
us no trouble at all; they used to spend all their
time botanizing and sketching. On this afternoon Mrs. Allan went down to the ravine below
to sketch some peculiar bit of rock scenery. I
think all ladies sketch when they travel, some
more and some less. But Mrs. Allan could sketch
and paint really well, and often went off alone
short distances while her husband stayed to chat
with me. She had been gone about twenty
minutes when we were startled by a most awful
piercing shriek—another, another, and another—
and then all was still again. Before the first had
died away Allan and I were running at full speed
towards where we judged the shrieks to have come
from. Fortunately we were right. Down there,
a bit to the right, we came upon a fair-sized pool,
on the surface of which Mrs. Allan was still floating. In a few seconds we had her out and were
trying restoratives; and on detecting signs of returning life we carried her up to the waggons.
When she became conscious she started up with
oh! such a look of horror and fright. I'll never
forget it! Seeing her husband, however, and

holding his hand, she became calm again, and told us all about it.

'It seems she had been sitting by the side of the stream sketching the pool and the great perpendicular cliff rising out of it. The sunlight was playing on the water, silvering every ripple, and bringing out every detail of the rocks and foliage above. Feathery mosses festooned from cliff to cliff; maidenhair ferns clustered in every nook and crevice; the drops on every leaf and tendril glistened in the setting sun like a thousand diamonds. That's what she told us.

' She sat a few minutes before beginning, watching the varying shades and hues, when, glancing idly into the water, she saw deep, deep down, a sight that horrified her.

' On the rocks at the bottom of the pool lay the body of a gigantic Kaffir, his throat cut from ear to ear, and the white teeth gleaming and grinning at her.

' Instinctively she screamed and ran, and in trying to pass along the narrow ledge she slipped and fell into the water. Had her clothes not buoyed her up she would have been drowned, as when the cold water closed round her it seemed like the clasp of death, and she lost consciousness.'

' Well, what about the nigger ?' I asked, for

Harding had stopped with the air of one whose tale was told.

'Oh, he was dead right enough—throat cut and assegai through the heart. A fight, I expect.'

'What did you do?' I asked.

'Raked him out and planted him up here somewhere. Let's see—yes, that's the place'—indicating the pile of stones my brother was sitting on.

Jim got up hurriedly; perhaps, as he said, he wanted to look at the place. Yet there was a general laugh at him.

'Did you think he had you, Jim?' I asked innocently.

'Don't you gas, old chap! How about that bathe you were so bent on?'

Merciful heavens! The words fell like a bucket of ice-water on me. I made a ghastly attempt at a laugh, but it was a failure—an utter failure—and of course brought all the others down on me at once.

'The nigger seems to have taken all the bathe out of you, old man,' said one.

'Not at all!' I answered loftily. 'It would take more than that to frighten me.'

Now, why on earth didn't I hold my tongue and let the remark pass? I must needs make an ass of myself by bravado, and now I was in for it. There was a perfect chorus of, 'Go it, old man !' 'Now, isn't that *real* pluck ?' ' Six to four on the nigger !' ' I pet fife pound you not swim agross and dife two times.' This last came from the little French demon, and, being applauded by the company, I took up the bet. The fact is I was nettled by the chaff, and in the heat of the moment did what I regretted a minute later.

As I rose to get my towel I said with cutting sarcasm :

' I don't care about the bet, but I'll just show you that *everyone* isn't afraid of his own shadow ; though,' I added forgetfully, ' it's rather an unreasonable time to bathe.'

Here Frenchy struck a stage attitude, and said innocently :

' Ah ! vat a night foor ze bade !'

The shout of laughter that greeted this sally was more than enough to decide me, and I went off in search of a towel.

Harding, I could see, did not like the idea, and tried to persuade me to give it up ; but that was out of the question.

' Mind,' said he, ' I'm no believer in ghosts ; yet,' he added, with rather a forced laugh, ' this is the anniversary, and you know it's uncanny.'

I quite agreed with him, but dared not say so, and I pretended to laugh it off. I was ready in a

12

few moments, and then a rather happy idea, as I
thought, struck me, and I called out :

'Who's coming to see that I win my bet?'

'Oh, we know we can trust you, old chap!' said
Jim with exaggerated politeness. 'It'd be a pity,
you know, to outnumber the ghost.'

'Very well; it's all the same to me. Good-bye!
Two dives and a swim across—is that it?'

'Yes, and look out for the nigger !'

'Mind you fish him up !'

'Watch his teeth, Jack !'

'Feel for his throat, you know !'

This latter exclamation came from Jim ; it was
yelled out as I disappeared down the slope. Jim had
not forgotten the incident of the grave, evidently.

I had a half-moon to go by, and a ghostly sort
of light it shed. Everything seemed more shadowy
and fantastic than usual. Besides this, I had not
gone a hundred yards from the waggons before
every sound was stilled ; not the faintest whisper
stirred the air. The crunching of my heavy boots
on the gravel was echoed across the creek, and
every step grated on my nerves and went like a
sword-stab through me.

However, I walked along briskly until the
descent became more steep and I was obliged to
go more carefully. Down I went, step by step,
lower and lower, till I felt the light grow dimmer

and dimmer, and then quite suddenly I stepped into gloom and darkness.

This startled me. The suddenness of the change made me shiver a bit and fancy it was cold ; but it couldn't have been that, for a moment later the chill had gone and the air was close and sultry. It must have been something else. Still I went down, down, down, along the winding path, and the further I went the more intense seemed the stillness and the deeper the gloom.

Once I stood still to listen ; there was not a stir or sound save the trickling of the water below. My heart began to beat rather fast, and my breath seemed heavy. What was it ? Surely, I thought, it is not fright ? I tried to whistle now as I strode along, but the death-like silence mocked me and choked the breath in my throat.

At last I reached the stream. The path ran along the side of the water among the rocks and ferns. I looked for the pool, but could not see a sign of it. Still I followed the path until it wound along a very narrow ledge of rock.

I was so engrossed picking my steps along there that, when I had got round and saw the pool lying black and silent at my feet, I fairly staggered back with the shock. There was no mistaking the place. The pool was surrounded by high rocks ; on the opposite side they ran up quite perpendicularly to a good height. Nowhere, except the ledge at my feet, would a man have been able to get out of the water alone. The black surface of the water was as smooth as glass ; not a ripple or bubble or straw broke its awful monotony.

It fascinated me ; but it was a ghostly spot. I don't know how long I stood there watching it. It seemed hours. A sickening feeling had crept over me, and I *knew I was afraid.*

I looked all round, but there was nothing to break the horrid spell. Behind me there was a face of rock twenty feet high with ferns and creepers falling from every crevice. But it looked black, too. I turned silently again towards the water, almost hoping to see something there ; but there was still the same unbroken surface, the same oppressive deadly silence as before. What was the use of delaying ? It had to be done ; so I might as well face it at once. I own I was frightened. I would have lost the bet with pleasure, but to stand the laughter, chaff, and jeers of the others ! No ! that I could never do. My mind was made up to it, so I threw off my clothes quickly and came up to the water's edge. I walked out on the one low ledge and looked down. I was trembling then, I know.

I tried to think it was cold, but I *knew* it was not that. I stooped low down to search the very depths of the pool, but I could see nothing; all was uniformly dark. And yet—good God ! what was that ? Right down at the bottom lay a long black object. With starting eyes I looked again. It was only a rock. I drew back a pace and sat down. The perspiration was in beads on my forehead. I shook in every limb ; sick and faint, my breath went and came in the merest whispers. So I sat for a minute or two with my head resting on my hands, and then the thought struck me, ' What if the others are watching me above ?'

I jumped up to make a running plunge of it, but, somehow, the run slackened into a walk, and the walk ended in a pause near the ledge, and there I stood to have another look into the dark, still pool.

Suddenly there was a rustling behind me. I jumped round, tingling, quivering all over, and a pebble rolled at my feet from the rocks above. I called out in a shaky voice, ' Now then, you chaps ! none of that ; I can see you.' But really I could see nothing, and the echo of my voice had such a weird, awful sound that I began to lose my head altogether. There was no use now pretending that I was not frightened, for I was. My nerves were completely unstrung, my head was splitting, and my legs could hardly bear me. I preferred to face any ridicule rather than endure this for another

minute, and I commenced dressing. Then I
pictured to myself Jim's grinning face, Frenchy's
pantomime of the whole affair, Harding's quiet
smile, and the chaff and laughter of them all, and
I paused. A sudden rush, a plunge and souse,
and I was in. Breathless and gasping I struck out,
only twenty yards across; madly I swam. The
cold water made my flesh creep. On and on,
faster and faster; would I never reach it? At
last I touched the rocks and turned to come back.
Then all their chaff recurred to me. Every stroke
seemed to hiss the words at me, 'Feel for his
throat! Feel for his throat!' I fancied the dead
nigger was on me, and every moment expected to
feel his hand on my shoulder. On I sped, faster
and faster, mad with the dread of being entangled
by the legs and pulled down—I swam for life.
When I scrambled on the ledge I felt I was *saved!*
Then all at once I began to feel my body tingling
with a most exhilarating sense of relief after an
absurd fright, a sense of power restored, of self-
respect and triumph and an insane desire to laugh.
I did laugh, but the sepulchral echoes of my
hilarious cackle rather chilled me, and I began to
dress.

Then for the first time occurred to me the conditions of the bet : ' Two dives and a swim across.'
Now, this would have been quite natural in ordinary

pools—a plunge, a scramble on the opposite bank, another plunge, and back. But here, with the precipitous face of rock opposite, it meant *two* swims across and *two dives* from the same spot. But I did not mind; in fact, I was enjoying it now, and I thought with a glow of pride how I would rub it into Jim about fishing up his darned old nigger with the cut throat.

I walked to the edge smiling.

' Yes, my boy,' I murmured, ' I'll fish you up if you're there, or a fistfull of gravel for Jim and Frenchy—little devil! It'll be change for his fiver ;' and I chuckled at my joke.

I drew a long breath and dropped quietly into the water, head first; down, down, down—gently, softly. A couple of easy strokes and I glided along the bottom. Then something touched me. God in heaven! how it all burst on me at once! I felt four rigid fingers laid on my shoulder and drawn down my chest, the finger-nails scratching me. Instantly I made a grasp with both hands ; my left fastened on the neck of a human body, and my right, just above, closed, and the *fingers met* through the ragged flesh of a gashed throat.

I tried to scream—the water choked me. I let go and swam on, and then up. I shot out of the water waist high, gasping and glaring wildly, and then soused under again. As I again came up I

dashed the water from my eyes. I saw the surface
of the pool break, and a head rose slowly. Kind
Heaven! *there were two!* Slowly the two bodies
rose across the black margin where the shadow
ceased, full in the moonlit portion of the pool—
cold, clear and horrible in their ghastly nakedness.
And as they rose the murderous wounds appeared.
The dank hair hung over their foreheads; the
glazed and sightless eyeballs were fixed with the
vacant stare of death on *me*. One bore a terrible
gash from temple to eye, and lower down the bluish
red slit of an assegai on the left breast.

On the other was one wound only; but how
awful! The throat was cut from ear to ear; the
bluish lips of the great gash hung wide apart
where my hand had torn them. I could even see
the severed windpipe. The head was thrown
slightly back, but the eyes glared down at me with
an awful stony glare, while through the parted lips
the teeth gleamed and grinned cold and bright as
they caught the light of the moon. One glance—
half an instant—showed me all this, and then, as
the figures rose waist-high, I saw one arm rigid at
right angles to the body from the elbow, and the
stiff hand that had clawed me. For one instant
they poised, balancing; then, bowing slowly over,
they came down on the top of me.

Then indeed my brain seemed to go. I struggled

under them. I fought and shrieked ; but I suppose the bubbles came up in silence. The dead stiff hand was laid on my head and pressed me down— down, down ! Then the hand of death slipped, and I was free. Once I kicked them as I struggled to the surface, and gasping, frantic, mad, made for the bank. On, on, on ! O God ! would I never reach it ? One more effort, a wrench, and I was out. Never a pause now. One bound, and I had passed the ledge ; then up and up, past the cliffs, over the rocks, cut and bleeding, on I dashed as fast as mortal man ever raced. Up, up the stony path, till, with torn feet and shaking in every limb, I reached the waggon. There was an exclamation, a pause, and then a perfect yell of laughter. The laugh saved me ; the heartless cruelty of it did what nothing else could have done—it roused my temper ; but for that, I believe I should have gone mad.

Harding alone came forward anxiously towards me.

'What's the matter ?' he asked. 'For God's sake, what is it ?'

The laugh had sobered me, and I answered quietly that it was nothing much—just a thing I would like him to see down at the pool. There were a score of questions in anxious and half-apologetic tones, for they soon realized that something was wrong ; but I answered nothing, and so they followed me in silence, and there, on the oily, unbroken surface of the silent pool, floated in grim relief the two bodies. We pulled them out and found the corpses lashed together. At the end of the rope was an empty loop, the stone out of which I must in my struggle have dislodged. Close to the nigger we laid them, with another pile of stones to mark the spot ; but who they were and where they came from none of us ever knew for certain.

The week before this two lucky diggers had passed through Newcastle from the fields, going home. Four years have now passed, letters have come, friends have inquired, but there is no news of them, and I think, poor chaps ! they must have ' gone home ' by another route.

TWO CHRISTMAS DAYS.

It was Christmas Day at New Rush—the Christmas of '73. No merry peals rang out to celebrate the occasion—there were no bells. The streets were not decorated with festoons or bunting—there were no streets to decorate. The usual lot of church-goers : men in broadcloth, women in gay colours, children neat and spotless, Prayer-book in hand—these were not the features of the day. There was no broadcloth, there were no women, there was no church—only long straggling rows of white tents, only a lot of holes of various depths and a lot of heaps of débris, only a lot of men in flannel-shirts and moleskins, broad brimmed hats and thick boots, the bronzed, bearded, hardy pioneers of the Diamond Fields. They had no church, but they could celebrate Christmas as well as those who had. There was a function which appealed to their feelings as Britishers—a popular, time-honoured function, whose necessary auxiliaries were at hand.   They could not go to church, but they *could* get drunk ; and they did.

All through the day the songs and cries and curses of the celebrants bore ample testimony to their devotion. The canvas canteens were crowded, and the bare spaces around them were strewn with empty bottles and victims of injudicious zeal. Within and without the one never - ending topic was diamonds ; diggers backed their finds for weight or colour, shape, or number.   Fortunes were held in clumsy, grog-shaken hands, and shown round as ' last week's finds '; all was clamour, festivity, and drink.

And this was Christmas Day ! And the same sun that blazed down so fiercely on the drinking, and scorched the unconscious upturned faces of the drunk, shone softly on the dark hedges and snow-clad meadows of old England.   It saw the fighting and drinking of a turbulent New World and the peace and quietness of a respectable Old one.   It saw the adventurers seeking fortune and the homes for which they worked.   And across six thousand miles of land and ocean it looked down alike on the men who waste or struggle and the women who wait and pray.

In a fly-tent, away from the noisy portion of the camp, sat John Hardy—sober.   Out of sorts, out of heart, and dead out of luck, he had neither the means nor the inclination to get drunk. Ten months on the fields had about done for him. Other men came with nothing; they had made fortunes and left. He came with a few hundreds, the proceeds of the sale of his farm and stock. He had sacrificed everything to come to this El Dorado—and now! Now the farm was gone and the money too. Bit by bit it had slipped away. The last thing to go was the cart and mule; he had managed to keep those till yesterday, but the grub score had to be met—one must live, you know—and the old mule and cart went the way of the rest. Last night he had changed his last fiver and paid his boys. Now all he had in the world was a bit of ground (thirty by thirty), a few old picks and shovels, two blankets, and a revolver.

All through the day he had heard the noise of shouting and singing, but it awoke no responsive chord. Every burst of merriment jarred on him. The first man he had met had smilingly wished him a merry Christmas. Great Heaven! was the man a fool, or was it a devil jeering at him? Merry! Ay, with black ruin on him, his hopes blasted and his chances gone. And this was Christmas, when human beings were gasping and blistering between the parched plain and the blue sky, where a fierce relentless sun blazed down

upon them. Everything mocked him. Truly,
when a man is down, trample on him! When it
comes to this, that his own feelings are a hell to
him, the more material things matter little. There
is a limit to mental as well as physical pain ; the
mind becomes numb and the feelings spent. But
Hardy had not yet come to this, and he felt
acutely the sarcasm on his own fate that this
Christmas Day presented.

At sunset he went out to take a last look at the
hole that had swallowed up his all. Indeed, it was
a poor exchange for the grand old farm and the
cattle and sheep and horses, and, above all, the
home that his dead wife had made a heaven of for
the five years of their married life. For himself
he cared little, but his little girl—her child !—
whom he had left behind with friends ! In his
mad speculation he had robbed her—his darling,
the one loving memento of his dead wife! Well,
to-morrow at sunrise he would take the £15 for
the claim, and hire himself out as a miner to the
new owner.

The setting sun glinted over the workings and
shed its golden light on the mine, ribbed out by
roads and divisions, all in little squares like the
specimen-cases in museums. There were hundreds
of those squares, and his was *one*, and a worthless
one at that. Yes, he would take the £15, and

lucky to get it, for every man in camp knew he had not found a stone worth mentioning.

For over two hours he sat in the little low tent ; a dusty lantern dangled from the ridge-pole and shed its weak, uncertain light around. His supper he had forgotten, and he sat at the rough packing-case table, his forehead resting on his arms, inwardly and silently cursing his luck and himself and the place with the bitterest curses his mind could frame. A revolver lay on the table before him—a grim sort of companion for a ruined man.

Presently a step came along the path—the step of one walking cautiously to avoid the scores of tent-lines and pegs that were stretched and stuck in every direction. As the step came closer Hardy looked up, and a head was thrust through the flap of the tent.

' I was taking Jack Evans home and he asked me to give you this. It came yesterday, but he's been spreeing and forgot it.'

The man stepped in and tendered a square envelope, and stood silent.

' Won't you sit ?' asked Hardy, scarcely glancing at him as he pushed an empty gin-case forward.

' Well, just a minute, thanks.'

The young fellow sat down and watched Hardy in silence. The latter took the letter mechanically, but brightened up instantly as he saw the writing.

Gently and carefully he opened it, and from the
envelope came a cheap Christmas card of flowers
done in flaming colours—common and garish. That
was all! No letter, nothing else. On the back
was written, ' For dear Father, from his little girl,
Gracie.'

For a moment Hardy looked at it steadily, and
then the hard sunburnt face softened, the mouth
twitched once or twice, and two tears trickled
slowly down and dropped on the card. The man's
head was lowered slowly until it rested on his
arms again, and for a couple of minutes there was
silence in the tent. The bitterness, the loneliness,
the desolation were gone from his heart. What no
reverses could bring about, and what no philosophy
could resist, was done by a cheap, tawdry Christmas card sent by a child.

Presently he looked up and reached a small
framed photograph from above his bed.

' It is from my little girl,' he said, and handed
the card and photograph to the youngster.

The boy looked at them. The photograph was
that of a child of about eight, with a rather
pleasant expression and large, wondering, honest-
looking eyes. He looked at it closely for a minute
or so, and nodding kindly once or twice, handed
it back without a word. As Hardy turned to
replace the photograph the youngster leant forward

quickly, took up the revolver, and slipped it into his pocket.

He had been gone ten minutes or so, when again a step came along; the flap was lifted, and without a word the youngster re-entered, drew the gin-case up opposite Hardy, and took a long steady look at him. To Hardy's ' Hallo ! what's up?' he returned no direct answer, but his eyes, which before had borne a calm, uninterested look, now shone with an eager brilliancy that could not fail to attract attention. His olive-brown face was pale, almost white now, and when he did speak it was, though slowly, with evident excitement, and he coughed once or twice as if feeling a dryness in the throat.

' The chaps say you are broke,' he said.

' Dead broke !' Hardy replied wonderingly.

' Have you anything left?'

' Nothing—absolutely nothing !'

' Where's your claim ?'

' Going to-morrow !'

The youngster shook his head and smiled faintly. He was so evidently in earnest that Hardy submitted in simple wonder to the cross-examination.

' Have you found any stones ?'

' Not five pounds' worth in ten months !'

' Where are your boys ?'

' Gone. I paid them off yesterday.'

13

'No, they're *not* gone. Look here,' he added
more quickly, ' when I was here before I took your
revolver. You see, it looked to me as if you
meant using it. Here it is. You can use it now
on someone else.' The youngster leant forward
and spoke lower and faster. 'When I left you
I walked along the old path a bit, but my sight
was spoilt by the candle here and I got off the
track. I stood for a minute, and then heard some
Kaffirs talking, and I went towards the sound. I
called to them, but they didn't hear me; and I
was walking up closer when I caught something
that made me listen all I knew. I heard more
and crept closer. I got quite close up and looked
through the grass. There were five boys sitting
round a stump of lighted candle ; there was a bit
of black cloth before them, and they *were counting
diamonds!* There was a mustard-tin full. I crept
back about twenty yards and called out. The
light was blown out at once, and when I called again
one boy came out. I asked him who was his baas,
and he brought me to your hut.'

Hardy sat dazed for a moment. Mechanically
his hand closed on the revolver that was placed in
it, and then, rising, he followed the lantern which
the youngster had taken.

They entered the hut and caught the boys in the
act of dividing the spoil. They found the mustard-

tin full, and on each of the Kaffirs a private supply hidden there from his mates.

John Hardy slept that night as those sleep who have borne their burden and have reached the place of rest. And he saw a picture in his dreams. The canvas tent was a palace of white marble, and as he lay there things of beauty were strewn around him; but, surpassing all these, there hung in mid-air before him a wreath of bright and many-coloured flowers, more lovely than any he had ever seen; and within its circle was the face of a child, and above it all there was a line of little crooked writing, and the letters, which stood out in shining gold, were, ' For dear Father, from his loving little girl, Gracie.' That was John Hardy's Christmas dream.

*   *   *   *   *

In 1885 New Rush and Colesburg Kopje were names well-nigh forgotten, and there reigned in their stead Kimberley and its neighbouring camps. In proportion as the tented camp had grown into a great city, in proportion as the puny diggings had become a mighty mine, in like proportion had men and things altered; and even so had John Hardy thriven and prospered. One stroke of luck had placed his foot on the first rung of Fortune's ladder, and a cool shrewd head had done the rest. Hardy the digger, in his little canvas tent, was no

more, and in his place stood John Hardy, Esq.,
capitalist, speculator, director of companies, etc.
But the change, after all, was no change at all: the
man was the same, and the very traits which, with
his fellow-diggers, had stamped him as a white
man, now won him the respect of a different class.
Calm and self-contained, straightforward and in-
corruptible, he was as popular as such men can be.
In one particular especially was he unchanged.
His ' little girl ' was still his ' little girl,' in spite
of the fact that she was now over twenty.   During
ten years he had not lost sight of her for a week,
and in all the world he had not one thought, one
wish, one desire, that had not for its aim her
happiness and pleasure.   On the banks of the
Vaal River he had made his home.   It was an
old farm, with great, big old trees and shady
walks and green hedges, and there was an
orange-grove that ran down to the river-side, and
a boat on the water, where one could glide about
breathing the breath of the orange - blossoms.
Here Hardy spent nearly all his time, perfectly
happy and contented in the society of his ' little
girl.'

But even so there were crumpled rose-leaves in
John Hardy's bed.   The first was the thought that
some day she, his child, would love someone else,
and he who had idolized her all his life would be

superseded by a stranger of whose existence even
she was not yet aware. The other was a now
half-forgotten ungratified wish—the wish to find
the youngster who had done him such service
twelve years before. Every effort had failed, every
expedient proved fruitless. Not knowing his
name, having hardly noticed his appearance, what
chance was there of finding him? He had but one
guide. Leaning across the rough table in the weak
uncertain light of the lantern that night, he had
looked full and fair in the youngster's eyes, and
he thought he would know them. If ever he got
the chance of looking into them again, he would
make no mistake. He remembered their colour,
he remembered them dark and dormant when he
brought in Grace's letter ; he recalled them again,
lustrous and expressive, when he returned to the
little hut, and could see them now, warming,
quickening, brightening, till they flashed with
excitement as he said, ' They were counting
diamonds.' Every little incident of that night
was burned into his memory, but of the general
appearance of the boy he knew nothing. He had
not seen his figure, standing or walking, except
for an instant, and that when he was paying little
heed. He had not seen his face, except in one
position—full—and that so close as to miss the
general impression. So many years had passed

without a sign or clue that Hardy had long given up all hope of discovering his friend, and, indeed, he seldom thought about him now.   When the thought did recur to him it came more as a regret that he had not found him than as a hope that he would.

It was Christmas Eve, and John Hardy was going into camp to arrange matters so that he would be free from all business during the holidays and could spend his Christmas and New Year at home undisturbed.   The cart and grays had already disappeared over the rise.   Grace had waved her good-bye and wandered off into the garden.   There were the cheerful sounds of life about which seem peculiar to a bright summer morning.   The finks on the river, the canaries in the field, the robbers in the orchard, vied with each other in pouring out volumes of song, lavishly squandering the wealth of their repertoire, and, as a sort of accompaniment to them, came the distant and pleasantly monotonous cackling of hens. Every variety of time, key, and voice was there, and all in rivalry, yet forming together a drowsy harmonious symphony of peace.   Miss Grace wandered on, pruning here, plucking there, now stooping to see where the violets hid their heads, now running her hand lightly through the clusters of roses.   She made her way slowly towards the house, looking fresh and bright in her white dress. The brown-holland apron was caught up and filled with bright azalea blossoms. The broad-brimmed garden-hat had slipped back, showing waves of golden hair; her lips and fingers, too, were stained with mulberries; at her breast was a bunch of violets to match the eyes above them. Altogether, she was not the least attractive part of the picture that summer morning, and probably she knew it. From the broad-flagged stoep of the house to the gravel sweep in front there were a dozen or so steps, and on the top step of all Miss Grace turned and stood. The gravel walks and big trees, the flower-garden wildly luxuriant, the orange-grove, and beyond them the reach of river, looking placid and blue in the morning sunlight, all made up a delightful picture; and she, with her snow-white dress and bright-coloured flowers, looked and enjoyed it. The gentle morning breeze, laden with the scent of flowers, played on her cheeks and just stirred the feathery golden hair on her temples as she stood there.

Presently someone, a stranger, rode up and, dismounting, led his horse to the foot of the steps, and, raising his hat slightly, asked for Mr. Hardy.

'He has just gone into Kimberley. He is not half an hour gone,' Miss Grace replied.

The man looked disappointed.

' That *is* unfortunate.   I have come a long way to see him.   I *must* see him.   When will he be back ?'

' This afternoon or this evening, I hope ; but possibly not until to-morrow morning.   But won't you come in and rest a little ?'

The man gave his horse to a boy and walked slowly up the steps.   For some moments he made no reply, and at last, looking at her in an abstracted kind of way, apparently without really seeing her, muttered :

' Well, that *is* awkward !'   He paused again, deep in thought, and, seeming to arrive at some con- clusion, he said, ' Miss Hardy, I *must* see your father ; it is a matter almost of life and death, and I am almost certain to miss him if I follow him now.   Will you allow me to wait until he returns ?'

' I shall see Mr. Whitton, my father's agent, at luncheon, and if he can put you up you are very welcome to stay.'

The stranger bowed, inwardly a little amused perhaps at Mr. Whitton's position in the matter.

Miss Hardy suggested that possibly he had not yet breakfasted, and as the surmise proved entirely correct he was left to entertain himself while she went off to give the necessary orders.

Breakfast over, the young man returned to the

stoep, and in an enclosed portion of it discovered Miss Grace among the ferns and hot-house plants. For some minutes after the first few remarks he watched in silence, and then, as she paused to study the effect of a rearrangement in a small basket of ferns, he asked quietly :

' Are you Miss Gracie ?'

She looked up quickly, flushing a little, and then said coldly:

' Yes, I am Miss Hardy.'

' I mean no impertinence, Miss Hardy. I asked if you are Miss Gracie because I heard of you by that name twelve years ago.'

' Indeed! Then you are an old friend of my father's ?'

' Well, yes, I believe he would consider me so. But I should have told you my name before this. Pardon the omission. Ansley it is — George Ansley.'

' Ah—Mr. Ansley! Yet I don't remember ever hearing him speak of you. But be sure of this, if you were his friend then, you will be his friend now. He does not forget old friends. Let me see. Twelve years ago. Those were the early days— those were his hard times when you knew him.'

' Yes, he was down then—very down ; and I am very glad he has prospered. No man better deserved it.'

The girl's eyes grew a little misty—this was her
weak point. She looked up at him, saying simply:
' Thank you.'

Ansley smiled slightly, and said :

' There was a photograph of you that he had
then. A little girl in short dresses, a very serious,
earnest-looking little girl—all eyes. I can remember wishing to see you then. I wanted to see
if your eyes really looked like that. They *do*,
you know. But, still, I can't imagine that you
are his " little girl." '

Miss Grace laughed and blushed a good deal under
the scrutiny and criticism, and suggested good-
humouredly that if he would go with her she would
show him the original photograph, and he could
satisfy himself on that point.

From one of the drawing-room tables she took a
folding frame made to hold two photographs, and
pointing to the right-hand one, handed it to him.
After a full minute's close inspection, Ansley
looked up, smiling gravely at the girl.

' There is no mistaking it,' he said ; ' that is the
photograph. I would know it anywhere. It
made a great impression on me when I first saw it
on account of a little incident that was in a sort of
way connected with it.'

' What was that ?'

As she asked the question he glanced from the

photograph to the other side of the frame, where
there was a little faded, old-fashioned Christmas
card.   As it caught his eye a half-suppressed
exclamation escaped him, and, oblivious of the
girl's presence, he drew the card out and read the
writing on the back; and then, glancing out
through the open window, he thought of how he
had first seen it.

As Miss Grace looked at him, she saw that his
brown sunburnt face looked a little lined and care-
worn.   Under the dark moustache the mouth
drooped rather sadly at the corners, and the eyes
were large and sad too just now.   She watched
him for a little while, and then, interrupting his
thought, said gently :

' Well, Mr. Ansley, I am waiting to hear the
incident of which I was the unconscious heroine.'

' A thousand pardons.   It was thinking of that
very incident that made me forget your question.
It cannot be an accident that those two cards are
in the same frame.   Of course, you must know the
history ?'

' Of course, *I* do ; but surely you cannot ; why,
the Christmas card it is impossible that you could
have seen.'

' No, not impossible, Miss Hardy.   It was I
who brought it to your father the night he found
the diamonds !'

The girl stood before him, hands clasped, and amazed. Wonderingly she looked at him, and the more she looked the more she wondered. How utterly different from what she had fancied! In her mind's eye she had seen a tall, awkward youth, loose-jointed and rough, silent and stupid, and here was the real Simon Pure, tall and slight, certainly, but supple and well-knit, quiet and courteous.

'Well, this is wonderful!' she exclaimed at last in helpless amazement; and then her face flushed with generous enthusiasm. 'Oh, Mr. Ansley, you don't know what pleasure, what happiness this will be to my father! You don't know how he has longed to find you. This will be the happiest Christmas he has ever spent.'

'Do you really think he will be glad to see me?'

'Oh, you don't know him if you can ask such a question. But why did you never come to us before?'

'Because I never wanted his help before, and I could not have refused it. He is the only man in this world from whom I would ask help, and I have come to ask it now. It is no trifle. It will be the hardest task he has ever had.'

'Whatever it is, Mr. Ansley, if he can do it he will. I would pledge my life on that. He owes you much, and I owe you what I can perhaps never in all my life repay. At least, you will let us be your friends.'

She extended both hands to him as she spoke. The soft firm touch of the girl's hands sent a pleasant tingle through him. It was genuine. It made him feel that this time he had fallen amongst friends. A feeling that he had never known in his life came over him, the feeling that there was a home where he would be always welcome, and that there were two people who would always be genuinely glad to see him.

The first surprise over, she made him recount most minutely every detail of that Christmas night. He told how the letter had been entrusted to him for delivery by the tipsy digger, and every little incident up to the finding of the diamonds.

'When we found the tin full,' he said, 'we were so excited that we thought very little of the boys. We searched them one by one and passed them behind us. I had passed the last, when I turned and found your father standing by me looking helpless and dazed, instead of guarding the door, as I thought he was doing. I looked round, and saw that the boys had bolted, so I took the packets we had found on them and put them down on the piece of oilskin with the tin. I thought it best then to leave him to himself, and as he stooped slowly to pick up the diamonds I stepped out of

the hut and went home. I should have seen him
the next day, I am certain, but when I got home
I found my father and a digging friend mad with
excitement about a new find some thirty miles
off. We started for the place that night, and did
not return for some months.'

'But how was it you did not meet him even
then ?'

Ansley laughed, as he answered hesitatingly :

'Well, Miss Hardy, the fact is, I did often meet
him ; but I was a youngster then—very foolish,
and sensitive, and proud in my silly boyish way,
and though I knew well and often heard that he
wanted to find me, I could not bring myself to
go up to him and say, " I am the man who saved
your fortune for you." It seemed to me I might
as well have said, " What do you mean to pay
me ?" I could not do it. And though I knew,
too, that he could not possibly recognise me from
the very imperfect view he had of me in the dark
little tent, yet when I met him in camp I used to
turn away from him and feel hurt and sick and
sore that he did not know me. Then a little later,
as you know, he left Kimberley, and was away for
a long, long time, and so it has been during twelve
years. He has been much away, and so have I,
and although I have often seen him, we have never
actually met. Once in London I would have

spoken to him. I was then, as I thought, a rich man, and I could afford to speak without fear of being misunderstood, but I missed him. I wish to God I had not, Miss Gracie ; I wish I had met you both then. Nothing has gone well with me since. Bad luck has followed me and all connected with me since then. It is the last and worst stroke that has brought me here.' He looked into the lustrous eyes and sympathetic face of the girl, and added, half playfully, half sadly : ' I wish I had met you before ; I believe you would have changed my luck. Do you know, I think you are one of those who bring good luck. You have a good influence —I can feel it.'

' If I have '—and the girl laughed brightly—' I mean to exert it from this very moment. Firstly, then, you must get out of the blues. Secondly, you must make up your mind to stay till my father returns ; and thirdly, you will have to submit with the best grace possible to the infliction of my company while I show you the sights and do the honours of our home.'

Whatever sacrifice of personal feelings Ansley may have made in the cause of gallantry was borne with Spartan fortitude and concealed with admirable skill; in fact, a casual observer would have been inclined to think that he rather liked it.

If he was not very talkative and lively, he made
up for it by being an admirable listener—one of
those listeners whose very look is full of quiet and
intense appreciation of all that is said. She was
content to play the cicerone, and it pleased him too,
and so the morning passed.

She took him through the grounds, idling along
amongst the summerhouses and trellised rose-walks,
telling him of their life there, of their plans, of her
own life during the years that had passed since he
first heard of her—in fact, all the reminiscences
which form the heart and charm of the meeting,
whether of old friends, or of the friends of old
friends, or of those who have a common bond of
sympathy wrought in a distant country or in a
troublous time.

Luncheon over, Miss Grace may have thought
she had answered the calls of hospitality, or she
may have been tired of his company, or she may
have thought that the change could do him good—
it is hard to say. But, any way, she handed her
guest over to the tender mercies of Whitton, and
for the rest of the afternoon, instead of her talk
and her company, Ansley had to put up with the
agent and his dissertations on farm prospects for
the coming season.

At about sundown, returning with Whitton from
an inspection of the stables, Ansley saw with no

little relief and satisfaction a slim figure in a gray dress moving about the lawn; and, leaving the estimable but prosy Whitton with the flimsiest of apologies, he joined his hostess.

'Really, Miss Hardy,' he said, coming up to her, 'I began to think you had vanished like the "baseless fabric." I was afraid you were going to leave me with Whitton for the evening as well.'

'Did you not enjoy his company, Mr. Ansley? I think him so entertaining and instructive,' she added demurely.

'Oh yes, indeed!' he answered hastily; 'but I mean, I think he knows too much for me. You see, I don't quite follow his theories—at least, some of them.'

'What a prettily - inferred compliment, Mr. Ansley!' and, making him a mock-curtsey, she added, 'Then you think *I* am sufficiently stupid to be entertaining?'

'Quite so, Miss Hardy—more of my own calibre, you know,' he returned, laughing.

'Thank you for that, too. My friend, you have a ready wit, and have got out of it better than you deserved; and, though you don't merit it, I mean to show you the river this evening—that is, if you are quite sure that you wouldn't prefer listening to Mr. Whitton.'

'Well, Miss Hardy, I could devote a lifetime to

14

agriculture, but the passion of my life is certainly
exploring. Your descriptions have so fired my
soul with enthusiasm and ambition that I am afraid
I shouldn't die happy if I didn't know the geography
of this part of the river.   In the cause of science,
let us go.'

The girl answered gravely :

' In the cause of science, we shall go.'

The evening was one of those stilly, cool
summer evenings so common in South Africa,
when the night seems full of still life ; the moonlight, strong and clear, has nothing sombre in it,
and the gentlest of cool breezes plays through the
leaves, bearing along with it the commingled scents
of all the blossoms.

As they walked down the gravelled path through
the orange-groves the crickets sang merrily all
around, and from the river came the sound of the
frogs—that most curious of all evening sounds.
From the house it sounded like one monotonous
roar, but as one drew nearer the river the individual voices could be distinguished, and every
note on the gamut was given by that orchestra.
Now and again, without any apparent reason, the
music would suddenly cease and a dead silence
ensue ; and then, doubtless at a signal from
the conductor, the whole band would strike up
again.

They strolled on down to the little jetty where the boat was moored, and helping his companion to the cushioned seat in the stern, Ansley pushed the little craft out and rowed lazily up in mid-stream.

From the river the groves and gardens showed up most distinctly, and over and beyond them the house was discernible under the huge trees that stood at the sides and back of it. The moonlight softened and silvered everything, and the scent of the orange - blossoms gave a dreamy, exquisite, impalpable finish to the night.

Pausing in midstream, Ansley asked his companion if she knew the song ' Carissima,' adding, ' You know, I think it must have been on such a night as this that he serenaded her in his boat. " The moonlight trembling on the sea," and " the breath of flowers," that he sings of are here, and " the orange-groves so dark and dim "—now all we want is the dreamy, distant sound of the " Vesper Hymn." Will you sing the song itself, Miss Hardy? That will be better than any " Vesper Hymn." '

She sang, as he asked, in a sweet, low voice suited to the song and the time and the surroundings ; and as the last call of ' Carissima,' so appealingly gentle, so soft and clear, floated away, he rested on his oars and watched her. Presently he said :

14—2

' There is, I think, no power so far-reaching, so
universally felt, as the power of music.   There is
none—excepting, of course, the magnetic power of
individuals over each other—which can so stir a
man's better nature.   It seems—and especially at
night—to elevate one's thoughts and hopes, to
strike a higher chord in human nature.'

' Yes, it is so.   It raises a feeling of devotion.
To me, it is the poetry of religion.'

And so they talked as the boat glided along ;
talked of the 'little things we care about,' which
are of no interest to anyone else, but which help
us greatly to know one another.   And the time
slipped quietly by, like the silent water moving to
the eternal sea.   Now and then there were scraps
of conversation, but more often the long silences of
content.   The girl lay back in the cushioned stern
trailing one hand in the water, barely cool after
the long summer day ; the man dipped his oars
now and again for the slowest, laziest of strokes,
and watched the blades glisten in the moonlight
and the diamond drops plash back on the shining
surface of the water.

Once or twice in the long silences Ansley had
roused himself, and half bent forward, as though
about to say something, but, changing his mind,
had taken a few lazy pulls at the oars and sent the
boat gliding along again.   But when they turned

to drift down stream again he shipped the oars,
and, after a little pause, said :

'If you do not mind, I should like to tell you
something of the business that has brought me
here. I want help for a friend, and I want advice—
your advice ! But, even apart from that, I should
like you to know.'

She answered promptly and truthfully :

'I should like to know, and oh! I would give
anything to help you !'

'I believe you would like to help me, Miss
Gracie ; indeed I do !' Ansley said, flushing a
little nervously. 'You can scarcely realize what
a difference this day has made to me. This morning I would have said I had but one friend in the
world, now I believe I have three ; and that makes
all the difference in the world to me. I confess I
did hope, though I was by no means sure, that
I could count on you and your father ; but I feel
more confident now. You have been more than
kind to me, and even if your father cannot help
me, yet for the welcome you have given me I
shall always count you as my friends.'

The girl, for answer, put out her hand to him.
The firm, honest grip, or the mere act perhaps,
seemed to confuse him for the moment, to put him
off ; and he sat silently looking down into the
hands which had just released hers. It was only

for a few seconds, however, and then he looked up at her and began abruptly :

'My other friend is a man named Norman. It is on his account that I have come here. He has been on the Diamond Fields off and on ever since they were found, and, like all others, he made and lost money alternately until about two years ago ; then the death of his father, with whom he had always shared interests, left him large holdings in several of the best companies. The business had been conducted under the style of Norman and Davis, and on the father's death young Norman left everything in the hands of Davis and went off on an eighteen months' trip. About six months ago he returned, and found that his position was not all that he had imagined it to be. He found Davis as a man a pretty wealthy man, but he found the firm of Norman and Davis as a firm an exceedingly poor one. The first glance showed him that Davis had worked with system. Whether the conversion had been effected during his absence only or during his easy-going father's lifetime it was impossible to say ; but the fact remains that the assets which he had looked upon as his had been converted to Davis's personal estate, and were as secure to him as law could make them. After some weeks of search, however, he found amongst his father's papers some-

thing which, though not in itself of great importance, yet gave him a good clue, and, making a
guess at the probabilities in the case, he wrote to
Davis demanding a full settlement in the matter of
certain shares which he could now prove belonged
to the firm.   To cut a long story short, Davis, not
knowing what documents had been discovered and
fearing a complete exposure, offered to compromise.
The more the one yielded the firmer was the other's
stand, and it was not till after several interviews
that any arrangement was come to.   Throughout
the whole business Davis's tone had been one of
contemptible cringing and meanness.   Pleading his
family, heavy losses, bad times, and a lot more in
that strain, he begged Norman not to be too hard
on him.   A day was appointed for final settlement,
when Davis would hand over some of his ill-
gotten wealth.   Norman called at the office as
appointed, and found his father's partner in a more
cheerful frame of mind, seemingly resolved to
accept the inevitable with the best possible grace ;
he treated the matter as a purely business trans-
action.   Finally, he asked Norman to leave the
documents with him to allow his clerk to take
copies of them.   If Norman would call back in
half an hour a lawyer would be in attendance, and
the business would be finally settled.   Norman
rose to go, and as he opened the door, Davis said

in a clear, low voice these words: "I am sorry
you have done it, Norman. I cannot have anything to do with that kind of business." As he
turned to inquire what Davis alluded to, the door
closed sharply, and he found himself in the pas-
sage and two strangers looking very hard at him.
There is no use telling you all the details, Miss
Gracie. I feel like a demon when I think of it
now. He was arrested and searched, and in one
of his side coat-pockets they found a small packet
of diamonds. This was proved against him at the
trial by the detectives, who swore also that they
had heard, as they stood outside the door, Davis
refuse to "have anything to do with that kind of
business." The clerk swore to Norman's several
visits, when he always refused to state his business, wishing to see Mr. Davis privately. Davis
himself of course with great reluctance gave evidence
against his late partner's son. He told how he had
of late been so pestered over this business that
he had at last given information in self-defence,
fearing that one day it would be discovered, and that
he, though wholly innocent, would be incriminated.
He hoped the Court would not be hard on the
prisoner, as he was sure this was his first offence,
and a lesson would suffice. The prisoner, he said,
was naturally a straightforward, honest man, and
he had never known anything against him before,

etc. The defence was characterized as a miserable failure, and the sentence on the prisoner was " seven years." I cannot tell you, Miss Hardy, half the horrors of that time. It was so terrible that I believe when the trial was over the certainty was no worse to him than the suspense had been. But the cruellest blow of all was to see friends drop away and sheer off when friends were most sorely needed. Norman said he had never seen the diamonds until they were found in his pockets by the detectives, and he could only think it was Davis's fiendish device to place them there while they were talking over the documents in the office. This explanation was openly laughed at. However, the law did not take its course—whether it was an act of negligence or covert friendship it is hard to say—Norman himself does not know; but an opening occurred two days after the trial, and he took it. Next to him stood one of the police-inspector's horses, saddled and ready, even to the revolver in the holsters. The act was so sudden that no attempt at pursuit could be made till he was well away towards the border. Galloping along in the early morning, he met no one for some miles out of camp, until on nearing the border, on the road before him, and coming leisurely towards him, he saw another horseman alone. Slackening his pace to allay suspicion, it was only when close

up that he recognised his late father's partner—the
cause of his ruin—Davis ; and not until Norman
drew up before him did Davis recognise the man
whom he believed to be in gaol. Paralyzed
with fright, he sat his horse speechless and helpless. Norman rode up closer until their knees
touched, and taking one rein in his hand, he held
Davis's horse. " You see I'm out," he said curtly.
Davis, white and trembling, could not answer a
word. " Give me all the money you have—everything of value. It is all mine, and I want it."
The miserable wretch handed out all his money
and his watch, together with several diamonds,
only too probably the fruits of that early ride.
Then Norman spoke again, with, you might say,
pitiless hatred. " You know, Davis, what you have
done ! You know it is *worse* than death to me.
Death would have been a thousand times better.
You know—of course, a religious man like you must
know—that retribution means an eye for an eye;
but I will not be as hard on you as you were to
me. I cannot have your liberty, or your reputation.
I cannot break your heart; but I *can* shoot you,
and, by God, I will ! Don't whine, you cur—*I*
didn't, when you dealt me a worse blow. Stand
back and take it." There was a report, a scream,
and—Davis was settled with.'

Ansley stopped. Before him shone the lustrous,

anxious, frightened eyes of the girl. Her face was colourless, and her hands clasped tightly together. As he stopped there came from the closed lips a breathless whisper—' Ah, God !'

For a full minute he sat looking at her, expecting, hoping she would say more ; but what she had heard seemed to fill her with thoughts too full for words. She asked no explanation—no reason— she could see them all herself. For the present she cared no more about his friend's after-fate—the fatal scene seemed too complete of itself to admit of anything more.

He looked at her wistfully, and said in a husky, pleading voice:

' Nothing can justify that, Miss Hardy, I know : but before you judge him, before you refuse your sympathy and help, think of the awful trial ; think of the fiendish cruelty of the man who had ruined him ; and think of how they met.'

' My sympathy is stronger than ever,' she answered, looking up at him. ' It was a terrible revenge, but no one can say it was more than justice.'

The girl sat silent again, thinking on what she had heard. Ansley was silent, too, feeling a little sore and disappointed at what he thought her disapproval of his friend ; but in reality he was mistaken, and her sympathy was the deeper that

it was not expressed. Several minutes passed
thus before either stirred or spoke again. Then
Miss Hardy rose and gathered her shawl about
her, saying :

' Come, let us go home. I feel chilly, and oh! I
cannot bear to think that a human being's life
can be so spoiled, so utterly, irretrievably ruined.
It is too cruel. Indeed, it almost makes one
think that this world is not the work of a God of
Justice and Mercy. It is horrible! It frightens
one to think that misfortune can so single out one
man for persecution worse than death. We have
but one life—one short little life, to live, and then,
to think that, do what we can, that may be spoiled
for us for ever !'

' Do you think that his chance is gone, then—
gone for ever ? He is still young. Do you think
nothing can wipe it out ?'

' Why do you ask me ? You know it is a thing
one cannot outlive. What would it help that you
and I were his friends—you and I and father ?—for
I know it will be so. I would honour him for his
wrongs. I would be proud to be his friend. But
it would always hurt to feel the sneers and insults
levelled at him. Were they never so well hidden,
he would know that they were there. But, for
that very reason, I would be proud to take his
hand before all the world.'

Ansley's glance kindled with pleasure to see the girl's earnestness, and, as he looked at her, he thought again of the photo he had seen that night twelve years ago. The honest, fearless look of the child came back to him, and it seemed to him that the woman was that child—and something more.

As they reached the stoep she turned to him, standing on the bottom step, and said gently :

'You will pardon my thoughtless chaff about your melancholy, won't you? I did not know then, but now I understand.'

'Never speak of it, Miss Grace. I knew you well enough even then to not misinterpret it. However, we have finished with melancholy now, haven't we? Do you know,' he added, smiling up at her, 'that it is past twelve o'clock, and Christmas morning? Let me wish you every happiness and every blessing. I think you deserve them. I told you I thought you had a good influence, and were born to make others happy. Now I am sure of it. I can speak from experience, for I have felt happier to-day than for many a long day past.'

'If I am that, what are you? Why, you are a Christmas-box yourself. Remember, I have taken possession of you, and mean to present you to father to-morrow morning as my Christmas-box. In the meantime you are mine.'

'And right welcome is my fate, my lady. Good-night.' He held her hand lingeringly as he spoke, then slowly bent and touched it with his lips, saying, 'Good-night, Gracie, my good angel!'

There was a faint whisper, 'Good-night,' and she ran quickly up the steps and disappeared indoors.

* * * * *

The sun had barely risen when Ansley, restless, and anxious for Hardy's return, left his rooms. Whitton, the overseer, was starting on horseback to go his morning rounds, and Ansley, glad of any means of passing the time, accompanied him. For a couple of hours he rode along with the overseer, listening absently to his one theme of conversation, but as it neared breakfast-time he struck off by a cross-path and rode slowly in the direction of the house.

This Christmas morning Miss Hardy was unusually late, and at seven o'clock she was startled by hearing the sound of a cart on the gravel outside. Catching her father's voice, she hastened to dress, and in a few minutes was downstairs to meet him; but the servant told her that he had just ridden off with three others, and had left word that he would be back again shortly, and that she must not wait breakfast for him, as he had some most important business to attend to. Wondering much what business could have been important enough to take him away so suddenly, especially on a Christmas morning, Miss Grace resolved, at any rate, to prepare her surprise for him, and sent for Ansley. But he too had gone out with Whitton, and not returned yet; and she, none too well satisfied, had to be content with her own company.

Having been unable to get away again the previous day, and having resolved to spend Christmas Day with his daughter, Hardy had left Kimberley long before dawn that morning. Driving along as he neared home, Hardy presently heard the sound of horses' hoofs coming on fast behind him, and, looking round, he saw two men ride up. One was a neighbouring farmer with whom he was slightly acquainted, and the other a stranger to him. The farmer told him hurriedly that Norman, the escaped I.D.B. convict, highwayman, murderer, and horse-thief, had been seen in the vicinity, and the detectives—pointing to his companion—were out after him. Hardy could give them no information, having just come out of Kimberley himself, and they were in the act of parting when another horseman came up—the second detective—with the news that he had seen Norman within the last half-hour, but, as he was well mounted and armed, had come for help.

People at a distance from the Diamond Fields cannot realize the hatred and contempt felt by the honest section there for the I. D. B.'s. It is the crime without parallel there, so that it is not to be wondered at that John Hardy instantly eagerly offered to join the party if they would accompany him to his house, a short way on, where he would leave the trap, and get a mount and arm himself.

Very few minutes elapsed before Hardy, the farmer, and two detectives were riding along fast in the direction in which Norman had been seen. A quarter of an hour's riding brought them to a rise at a considerable distance from the house, and, coming up first, Hardy, who had the best horse, signalled to the others to stop at once; and, dismounting at once, he crept up to watch the man who was riding slowly towards them.

Walking his horse leisurely along, Ansley was lost in the thought of his mission, in speculation as to how Hardy would receive it, and in the recollection of the previous day and evening. A happier look floated across his face as he thought of the young girl standing on the step above him, bathed in the soft moonlight, and his blood quickened a bit as he recalled the timid whispered ' Good-night.'

Suddenly a sense of danger came upon him, and, looking up quickly, he fancied he saw a man's head duck behind the ridge of hill. Reining up his horse instantly, he waited for a moment or so, watching intently and warily the while. Then, turning his horse's head, he rode towards another elevation, still watching the spot where the head had disappeared.

As he turned four horsemen dashed out, and scattering wide apart, rode towards him. With a muttered curse he tightened the rein and galloped off in an opposite direction. The man's face, soft and gentle as a woman's a moment before, grew hard and colourless; his mouth was set, and his eyes had a bright and wicked gleam in them.

Riding at their best over the rough ground, Ansley kept his lead easily; but Hardy drew away from the others, and they, seeing the chase tend towards the river, took a cut down to the nearest crossing, hoping to cut the pursued man off on the other bank, or take him while swimming the river, as he would have to do further down.

Seeing that Hardy was alone, Ansley slackened his pace till only thirty yards divided them, then, raising his open hand, called to him by name to stop. The answer was a revolver shot, closely followed by a second one, one of which whistled unpleasantly close. Seeing the man with whom he had to deal, Ansley let his horse go, and heading for the deepest part of the river, soon had a lead of several hundred yards. Plunging into the river, he swam his horse across, and as he neared the other side, Hardy, who had ridden his best in the last bit, came up to the bank and again fired at him. The bullet splashed far behind him, and, looking round, he saw Hardy force his horse into the stream to follow him.

As he reached the bank Ansley slipped off and loosened the girths, then turned and watched his pursuer. The look on his face was not good to see : the expression was vindictive and cruel, for the man's spirit was bitter with rancour. This was the sorest blow of all, that the man who owed him all he had—ay, even his life most likely !— should go out of his way to hunt him down and shoot him like a dog. As he watched, a gleam of light shot into his eyes and a smile flashed across his face, for Hardy's horse began to fail, and once or twice it stopped. The third time it reared up as it felt the spurs again, and Hardy, to save himself, swung off and tried to seize the pommel of the saddle; but the frightened, tired horse swayed round and, striking out wildly with his front feet, brought one down with a crash on Hardy's bare gray head. He was but twenty yards from the bank ; he made one weak effort to swim—a white upturned face showed for a moment and then disappeared.

Ansley stood perfectly still, the same smile still curling the corners of his mouth as he watched his pursuer go down. As the water closed over the pale set face, there came to him the faint, trembling sound of a whispered 'Good-night!' A run, a spring, a few quick strokes, and he had the drowning man by the collar and was dragging him out. A minute later he stretched him out on the bank, and waited for the effects of the blow to pass off.

'My God!' he thought, 'what a demon I have become! *Her* father and *my* friend, and I would have let him die because unknowingly he injured me. I *would* have done it, too, but for her!'

Hardy lay against a grassy bank, and at the first sign of returning consciousness Ansley leaned over him, chafing his hands and watching his eyes for a sign of recognition.

'Where am I?' he asked faintly. 'Ah, I see—I know!' And as he became stronger, he said : 'Ah, I have you ; you are my prisoner.' He made a feeble effort to grasp Ansley's throat, but, looking up into his eyes, he dropped back suddenly with a look of intense excitement, exclaiming eagerly : 'Man! Who are you? What is your name? Surely—surely you—the diamonds, you know, that Christmas night! I know you! Now I know you!'

Ansley looked at him steadily, and answered :

'Yes, Mr. Hardy, I am the man you have looked for. My name is George Ansley Norman. But just lie quiet for a few minutes, and you'll be all right. And then we'll get back to the house as soon as we can!'

Hardy closed his eyes and groaned aloud, but
after a pause said falteringly :

'Norman—but the convict—it *can't* be true ! my
God ! it *can't* be true !'

'It *is* true, Hardy. I am the convict, but there
was no crime. Between man and man, and by
the God above me, I am as innocent of it as you
are.'

'My boy, I believe you, and thank God for it,'
said the old man fervently, and the tears came into
his eyes as he added brokenly : 'And to think
that I tried to shoot you. *You*, my best of
friends—how can you forgive me !'

'Oh, that's all right now—you see, you didn't do
it, so it doesn't matter ; besides, you did not know
me, and how could you help it ?'

While they were talking, on the same bank, a few
yards off, the farmer and the two detectives were
crouching behind the bushes and creeping closer up.

Hardy spoke again, and a painful flush suffused
his face.

'It is the revolver you took from me that night.
I have kept it ever since. I might have shot you
with it. Take it from me again, and keep it, for
my sake !'

He handed it up as he spoke, and Ansley took it,
turned it round once or twice, and stooped to help
his friend to rise.

As he bent forward, a voice called out :

'Shoot quick, before he kills him !'

Two revolver shots rang together, and with a half-stifled cry, Ansley threw up his arms and dropped at Hardy's feet. A wild scream of agony burst from Hardy, and, weak as he was, his arms were in an instant round his friend.

'My God !' he cried wildly, 'you have murdered him ! Stand back ! leave him ! Speak to me, my boy, speak ! Where is it ? Where are you hit ?'

But Ansley shook his head ; his face was drawn and pale, and there was a look of intense suffering in his eyes. His voice quivered as he whispered slowly :

'Home — old chap — home — home — your daughter. I want—to—speak—to—her !'

So they carried him back as gently, as tenderly as they could—the man they had hunted and shot down; they laid him on the bed he had that morning risen from, and three of them left him. Whitton came in and would have tried to stanch the wound, but Ansley shook his head. In broken whispers he told Hardy how he had come to the house and waited for him ; how he had met Grace and told her all, excepting only his identity. He asked him to go to her and tell her that, and ask her would she come to him that he might see her once more.

The smile of welcome died on Grace's lips as she saw her father's face. He told her all as best he could. There was no attempt at control—it would have been useless. The sorrow-stricken old man, with sobs and tears, tried to break it to her, but it required little telling. Distracted with sorrow, remorse, and love for 'his boy,' as he called him, he blamed himself for it. He lost all control of himself.

'My child! my child! three times I tried to shoot him. I would have killed him; and yet I should have drowned, and he saved me—*he* saved me—the man I tried to shoot! He saved me—he was helping me, when—oh, my God!—they shot him through the back. Come to him, my child. Gracie darling, be brave and bear up. Oh, God! they have killed him!'

She went alone to where the dying man lay. Softly she entered, but he heard her, and his eyes followed her as she walked to his side. In silence she sat by him, taking his hand and stroking it gently. Slowly he was bleeding to death, yet his eyes were bright as he looked at her. He smiled at her and whispered huskily:

'I told you you were my good angel, and see, you have come to me. I *cannot* thank you enough. I asked for you because I want you to bid me one more good-night—good-night for ever. I want to hear you say I am your friend, of whom you are not ashamed. Can you say it, Gracie ?'

The words, the look, were too much. The girl's pent-up grief burst out in one heart-broken cry, and, falling on her knees, she kissed the hand of the man whom rightly or wrongly she honoured above all men.

*   *   *   *   *

This was their Christmas Day—twelve years since first their paths had crossed—twelve circles in the web of life! They were three units amongst the countless millions of the earth, and so, what of them ? What of sorrow ? What of death ? What of the wreck of new-born hopes ? For to the countless millions it is still A Merry Christmas!

THE END.

BILLING AND SONS, PRINTERS, GUILDFORD.

www.ingramcontent.com/pod-product-compliance
Lightning Source LLC
Chambersburg PA
CBHW020114030726
47498CB00006B/2107